Turn The Page

Turn your Pain into Power-
The story that transformed her into an unstoppable woman

DIVYA KESARKAR

BlueRose ONE

First Published in February 2023

ISBN: 978-93-5704-935-1

BLUEROSE PUBLISHERS

www.BlueRoseONE.com

info@bluerosepublishers.com

+91 8882 898 898

Cover Design:

Muskan Sachdeva

Typographic Design:

Rohit

Distributed by: BlueRose, Amazon, Flipkart

वक्रतुण्ड महाकाय सूर्यकोटि समप्रभ

निर्विघ्नं कुरु मे देव सर्वकार्येषु सर्वदा

"O Lord (Ganesha), who has a huge body, curved elephant trunk, and whose brilliance is equal to billions of Suns,

May always remove all obstacles from my endeavors."

Meaning: It is the famous 'shloka' for Lord Ganpati or Ganesha. Ganesha is the first to be worshiped among all the gods in Hindu mythology. He is known as the God of prosperity and wisdom and is believed to remove all obstacles, bestow happiness, and spread peace in the lives of his followers.

I am an ardent follower of Ganesha, my guiding light and savior. I do not wish for anything but his blessings to be showered upon me.

II Ganapati Bappa Morya II

Turn the Page

Turn your Pain into Power- The story that transformed her into an unstoppable woman

DIVYA KESARKAR

FOREWORD

This is a work of non-fiction. This story is based on actual events in the author's life that transformed her life. Anay, Meera (the narrator of the story), and their son Abeer are the fictitious characters created by the author. The locations used are from the author's personal life. Any resemblance to events, locations, or people is purely coincidental. The author has obtained the required permission to include the names of the significant people involved in the creation of this book in the acknowledgements.

Love is a feeling if you understand it... a joke if you do it... a world if you create it... a faith if you act it out. What happens is already written in our destiny and no one can change it. To me, my parents are my first love.

The book is dedicated to my parents. They are crucial to the success of the book. This journey would not have been possible without their ongoing and consistent support.

PREFACE

Because writing is one of my passions, I turned to it whenever life took its toll on me, and it turned out to be a watershed in my life; something that happened without my ever imagining it. That's when I decided to write my story, to create a narrative addressing the issue of domestic violence and expressing the problems I experienced while going through the agony of separation and loss on multiple levels, and everything gradually came together as I wrote about the events and sensations I envisioned.

Miracles, I believe, exist.

What you do with the possibilities that life throws at you is all that matters. What I believed in was to just keep doing your best in every circumstance. Also, I wanted to write it for all the people who take such incidents lightly with the fear of "**log kya kahenge?**" keeping it hidden for years, enduring such injustice and becoming adherent to the agony, making themselves immune to pain and sorrow.

I wanted to be among those ladies who have been an inspiration to me because they have gone through such tough times and have managed to come out clean, and I look up to them for having the guts to cope with harsher instances than mine and dealing with them elegantly, as well as being strong enough to give back to those who maltreated them.

Do not be a victim of domestic violence; it is sometimes unintentional and arises as a result of tension, lack of communication, or lack of courage to express one's genuine sentiments, disturbing a relationship that is not supposed to be shattered. Alternatively, if you know someone who is suffering and living in a similar position or going through violence, please support them in such instances by getting help from police, your loved ones, and family members rather than tolerating and feeling guilty for speaking out against such incidents. Men are not always at fault, it may also be women; I'm not generalizing here, that's why I am using the word "**cases**".

I do not wish for Meera and Anay's scenario to be used to define domestic violence. I also do not mean for Anay's persona to define the traits of the majority of abusers. Every circumstance is unique. Every outcome is unique. I chose to present my story, making it understandable in interpreting Meera and Anay's relationship, highlighting typical variables involved in abuse.

Where… Marlin was looking for Nemo and he was feeling really defeated, Dory said to him, "When life gets you down do you wanna know what you've gotta do? … Just keep swimming. Just keep swimming. Just keep swimming, swimming, swimming.

AUTHOR

<u>Note:</u>

<u>Assault</u>

Is the act of inflicting physical harm or unwanted physical contact upon a person or, in some specific legal definitions, a threat, or attempt to commit such an action. It is both a crime and a tort and, therefore, may result in criminal prosecution, civil liability, or both.

<u>Domestic Violence</u>

Violent or aggressive behavior within the home, typically involving the violent abuse of a spouse or partner.

"Not everyone will understand your journey. That's okay. You're here to live your life, not to make everyone understand."

- Dr. A.P.J. Abdul Kalam

CONTENTS

CHAPTER 1

THE BLACK DAY

Meera: Everyone Has A Story… Always Listen; Never Judge…

Two days before my brother's wedding. Everyone was pleased, enthusiastic, and eager. I was feeling conflicted. My heart was pounding with anxiety, agony, grief, and terror. My mind was jumbled. Greeting the guests while pretending to smile seemed like a burden that would weigh heavily on my heart. I was choking.

Unaware that it would be the final day I would see his face filled with hope before appearing in the court, Anay entered the room. He shocked my family and me by breaking the news about my jewelry being mortgaged, which was a very handy way for him to end the silence and set the record straight. My parents collapsed when they heard this and learned that I had been dealing with all of this for years without revealing anything to them. They were completely taken aback by the fact that they had been kept in the dark.

I confronted him that day. I had not allowed him to mortgage them. He had not changed despite all the lies I had put up with and all my demands for him to get his finances in line. I also thought that when his wrongdoings and lies were pointed out to him, he became overly hostile.

And Then…
FINAL ASSAULT!!!

[Streedhan includes all movable property, immovable property, gifts, etc. given to a woman by her parents prior to her marriage, at the time of her marriage, during childbirth, and during her widowhood.

A woman's husband may use her Streedhan during distress or emergency, but he is under moral and legal obligation to restore it or something equivalent to its value to his wife.

A woman has inalienable rights over Streedhan and she can claim it even after separation from her husband, the Supreme Court has ruled, saying that denying it would amount to Domestic Violence, making the husband and in-laws liable to face criminal prosecution].

I reached a breaking point and I could not take it anymore. I could not even be furious since it was beyond my comprehension. I was forced to make a decision. I reasoned that if my husband was going to assault me every time I asked him to return my jewelry, I couldn't risk being assaulted all the time. I didn't want to be abused again, nor did I want to give my husband any chance to do anything wrong with his life and then blame it on me.

I did all I could to help Anay —I offered him my love, my forgiveness, and numerous chances… requesting just one thing in return to maintain my value and the faith I had placed in him, only to discover that it was all a lie. I trusted and believed in him from the moment we walked down the aisle. Every relationship faces difficulties and challenges; in order to overcome those, both partners must have faith, trust, and transparency. We have had our disagreements, the ifs, and buts. I went overboard in believing his carefully painted falsehoods about the unknown and helping him solve all of his darn fu*king troubles and problems.

The biggest mistake I made is that I built my home with Anay. I decorated it with love; care and respect making me feel protected. I invested in him, and my self-worth is determined by how warmly this house greets me. However, I was unaware that when I built my home with him, I am giving him the power to mistreat me. I feel empty because everything that we had within us was because he was my home. I trusted him with pieces of us. The emptiness I feel does not mean I have nothing to contribute, or that I have nothing within me. It is just that I built my home in the wrong place. The love, caring, and respect I hoped for and expected were lacking or absent in our relationship. A true connection is when you can tell each other anything and everything. NO secrets NO falsehoods. He, on the other hand, kept me in the dark and killed me with suspense. I was aware that the relationship had become flawed, the cracks had formed, and that it needed care. He served it up with deception, lies, backstabbing, grief, and betrayal

I vowed to myself that there would be no turning back. My self-esteem was more important to me than the unhealthy relationship I was attempting to salvage. I trusted him until I left for Goa, but he made no effort to rebuild our broken trust. It left me with the deepest scar.

I was prepared to put up with a lot of nonsense from him, but it had reached an absurd level. I needed justice, and I deserved to completely stop tolerating it.

CHAPTER 2

HAPPY MOMENTS

PART I
⸌ HAPPILY EVER AFTER DAYS…!

It has undoubtedly been an emotional roller coaster. We've had some unforgettable experiences that we will always cherish.

The initial days of adjusting to the huge joint family were full of life and **hasi majak** and the attention and care I received were truly overwhelming. The kind of support Anay gave me in helping me to get to know everybody, introducing me to the giant joint family, and of course adding me to the **"family groups"** familiarizing me to a new environment and making me feel comfortable with everything.

I had never cooked before, but I was so convinced that I would study the tutorials on YouTube and pull it off… and I did that. My first ever shagun ki **'Kheer'** turned out to be the best and I received so much love and appreciation; I was truly happy that I could leave my mark on everybody's hearts, and then the next day, while making Sheera for Anay and myself, I told him *"I know everything, didn't I prepare kheer yesterday? It turned out to be great… You just wait and watch as I prepare the best sheera you're ever gonna have!"* and he was excited about having "**mere haath ka sheera**"

Everything seemed good until I started heating the ghee and sautéing the semolina on a medium burner for 6 to 8 minutes, stirring occasionally. After adding the milk, and I added water to match the quantity of semolina. That is where I went wrong, it did mix nicely and was cooked, but it became incredibly sticky. I added sugar, raisins, and cashew nuts, but it didn't taste like it should. Anay dubbed this 'Sheera' the 'Japanese Sheera', and we laughed heartily as he ate it gleefully for making me feel good and for my efforts and discreetly packed the remaining 'Sheera'. He instructed me to inform everyone that he had eaten it all and he snuck out of the house to give it to a stray dog or a cow so that it would not go to waste. I was moved by his gesture of showing his concern for rescuing me from the folks out there.

(I get teary thinking about how caring Anay was and what he had become. What had gotten into him? Or was he always like this?)

It was so nice. He used to go to work and I used to wait for him to have lunch. Not a single day went by that I didn't wait for him to have lunch. We always had lunch and dinner together, chit-chatting, making fun of each other, and making plans to go out on Sundays... making movie plans, going to places for dinners, or meeting his friends. It was insane going on late-night drives; I felt like a bird let free, truly enjoying the time I spent with him, and coming home late without having to answer anyone.

A few days later, we were deciding where to go for our honeymoon. We were making a list of destinations to visit. Anay didn't have a passport. We had decided to go to some international location; I insisted on him getting one because it is important to have a passport as you never know when you might need it; so he had gone to Mumbai because he was born in Dadar and he had to go there for his submissions and passport appointment; he was away for two days apparently and I missed him a lot, waiting for him to return as soon as possible.

Also, the "**Makar Sankranti**" festival (To celebrate the deity Surya (Sun). To mark the first day of the sun's transit into Makara rashi) was approaching; Anay completed all of the necessary procedures for his passport and came a day before Makar Sankranti. I was ecstatic on Makar Sankranti. It was our first festival together. My in-laws had purchased this '**Tilgul Dagine**' (The customary sugar jewelry, halwyache dagine, is crafted using sugar candies made out of roasted sesame seeds combined with sabudana and sugar powder) for me; I was set.

I enjoy festivals. I appreciate the meaning behind each celebration and the traditions that go along with it. I went to my room to change into my saree. It is customary to wear a black saree on that day, given to you by your spouse. I wasn't expecting one because I knew Anay was in Mumbai for his passport. When I opened my closet to get one, I noticed a saree bag on the shelf. I opened it to see a brand new black saree that Anay had bought me for Makar Sankranti. I leaped with delight. It was thoughtful of him to remember and get it when I least expected it. I kissed him and held him. I was excited to wear that saree; obviously, I didn't have the blouse sewn, but I managed to contrast it with another blouse and wore that saree, telling everyone at home that Anay had bought it for me. We took photographs of ourselves, where I was wearing my '**Tilgul Dagine**', celebrating the joyful start of our first festival together.

Now that the passport formalities had been finished and we were waiting for it to be couriered to us, we started planning our honeymoon getaway. We had to decide between Bali and Singapore, and Anay figured that I wanted to travel to Singapore, so we finalized to go to Singapore, and when I stated *"Malaysia is near Singapore, why don't we cover Malaysia too?"* He was like *"you are talking as if it's ek ke saath ek free kind of a thing"* and after a brief pause *"chalo thik hai, if you are saying so, let's do it."* and I made him include Malaysia in our itinerary.

Anay's passport arrived around 15-20 days later. Nowadays, getting a passport is simple. It was made under the Tatkal mode. I was overjoyed having my first international vacation with my better half.

I began preparing for the trip, from our bookings to coordinating the sites we wished to visit and I left no stone unturned in planning our honeymoon. I began shopping for myself and Anay. I made a day-by-day list of what he and I will wear based on our agenda. I arranged currencies, visas, and a shopping list for my family. Everything was double-checked. We only had to pack and go.

CHAPTER 3

SINGAPORE + MALAYSIA

Our flight was set to depart from Mumbai International Airport, so we drove to Mapusa, parked our car at my parents' home, said our goodbyes, and the driver dropped us off at the Goa Airport for Mumbai. When we arrived in Mumbai, we spent some time in the lounge area, taking pictures of ourselves. We finished all of the appropriate check-in processes, ate our meal, and waited for the clock to strike 1.40 a.m., though I don't recall the precise time the flight was scheduled. We were set for Singapore; it was a 10-day, 9-night package that included 5 nights in SIN(Singapore) and 4 nights in KUL(Kuala Lumpur, Malaysia).

DEPART BOM, ARRIVE SIN

We arrived early in the morning; the tour company had arranged for a pick-up, so our driver was waiting for us with a placard; we proceeded to our hotel, the ibis Singapore. We called our parents to inform them of our safe arrival and then relaxed for a while.

Our programme called for us to go on a Night Safari the same day we arrived. **Night Safari** is the world's first safari park for nocturnal animals. The wildlife park is home to wild creatures kept in the forest, and we were taken on an open jeep ride to see them. We had some incredible experiences that day.

We enjoyed a fantastic breakfast buffet the next morning. We appreciated a variety of options, which included croissants, fruits, boiled eggs, juices, and much more. It was just right. The watermelons were delicious.

Day 1 - Sentosa Island + Sentosa Wax Attraction - Madame Tussauds + Siloso Point Station. We had a terrific day riding the attractions, taking pictures, and getting soaked on the beach. We were totally exhausted.

Having had a fantastic day, I dozed off on Anay's shoulder in the van that arrived to pick us up; pleasantly smiling from within. We had no energy to even change our clothes when we arrived at the hotel, so we flopped on the bed and spent the entire night kissing and exploring each other.

Day 2 - We were running late for our sightseeing plans the following day. The receptionist woke us up with a call, and the van was waiting to pick us up. We got ready in a matter of minutes and headed to **S.E.A. Aquarium**, an unforgettable underwater experience. Labeled as the world's largest oceanarium, this place has unique marine habitats **and a Universal Studio**. It is a theme park located within the Resorts World Sentosa at Sentosa. It features rides, shows, and attractions as well as restaurants and street entertainment in each themed zone. It was an amazing day filled with a lot of fun, laughter, wild jokes, and chatter on the streets of Singapore. We loved getting clicked; we contacted our respective parents to share moments with them, making them glad that we were having a great time here.

That day, we finished early. We had plans for the 'NIGHT'. We arrived at the hotel, ate supper, and ordered beer. I fantasized about having my first alcoholic beverage with my husband. I was living my dream, and I had two tins since I was a beginner while Anay drank more. When we arrived at our room, the perfumed candles were lighted and there were rose petals on our bed. Our tour company had made the required arrangements because we were a honeymoon pair.

Our moods were lifted by the whole atmosphere. Anay hugged me from behind. I felt his warm breath on my neck as his arms wrapped around my waist; we were both breathing deeply. He kissed my earlobe gently and then began kissing me on the neck, getting close to my lips. I twisted over, grabbed his T-shirt, and drew him closer to me as he held my face in his hand. His other hand went down to unbutton my shirt, tossing me on the bed while we clutched each other. The foreplay was short-lived. We were soon stripped naked, with only the quilt covering our exposed bodies… We exchanged passionate kisses. The ecstasy had gotten into us, making our love intense and enticing; we couldn't keep our hands off one another; kissing, the moans and thrusts were working their magic until we were fully wet. That wasn't it… We bathed together, in the fragrance of body mists, turning on the heat in the jacuzzi, as we celebrated ourselves and our honeymoon night. It was amazing and sensual. We slept naked, snuggling up with the warm cuddly comforter, which gave us goosebumps and ecstasy the whole night.

Day 3 - We didn't want to get out of bed that morning, for obvious reasons related to what we had done the night before. We dragged ourselves to get ready for the city tour, which included the **National Orchid Garden**, **Little India**, and **Jurong Bird Park**. We were able to have some real Indian cuisine. We had butter chicken, roti, and rice. We liked the lunch and concluded our city tour.

Day 4 - It was a day for us to shop and explore on our own, so we strolled about, looking at things, window shopping, and doing some genuine shopping for our family before returning to our rooms and resting comfortably while also doing some '**love making**'. We had our flight arranged for the next morning. I was sad to say goodbye to Singapore yet I was also thrilled about Malaysia.

DEPART SIN, ARRIVE KUL

We arrived in the afternoon. Our driver dropped us off at our hotel, the Sentral Pudu, and informed us to get ready for the sightseeing plans, which included the **KL Tower** and **Twin Towers**, as well as an Indian supper put up by our tour company.

KL tower is the world's 7th tallest tower. We had gone in the night. The night views were equally incredible, but the best time to visit the tower is in the morning because you'd get to see a clear view of the city along with a nice breeze. The Petronas Towers, commonly known as the Petronas Twin Towers or KLCC Twin Towers, are 88-story supertall buildings in Kuala Lumpur, Malaysia, with a height of 451.9 meters. We ate some delicious Indian food that we had been craving and slept. It had been a long and tiring day.

Day 1 - Batu Caves; It was not initially part of the plan, but I insisted on going to Batu Caves and had it added, and there we were. The cave, dedicated to Lord Murugan, is one of the most prominent Hindu sanctuaries outside of India. It is the main point of Malaysia's Tamil celebration of Thaipusam. One must climb around 300 stairs to reach it, but it is worth seeing. We had coconut water on our way down those steps, we thoroughly enjoyed being there.

Day 2 - Sunway Lagoon. World's largest Surf Pool. Anay was going crazy hitting the beach and wanting to play. It was the best place to be. We were sunbathing and there was this area where there were tamed wild animals, so we were literally waiting for the tiger and the lion to wake up. They were sleeping. We took two to three rounds just to check if the lion had woken up, but had hard luck. Our driver drove us to see the **King's Palace** later that evening on our way back to our hotel.

Day 3 - Genting Highlands. Being on that cable car so high in the sky was one of the most thrilling sensations I'd ever had. I was hooked on Anay, and he had held me. We kissed each other, making it our most romantic cable car ride. It is undescribable. That night, while walking the streets of Malaysia, we stumbled upon Ali's biryani corner, where we enjoyed the most delicious biryani and returned to our hotel, calling for a love making session to commemorate our final night in Malaysia.

The next day, we had free time till the afternoon, but we didn't do much since we were too busy packing. We just bought chocolates because we had already bought enough stuff in Singapore for ourselves and our family. Our flight to Mumbai was planned for the afternoon. Our emotions were heavy as we said goodbye to the most unforgettable vacation. We had a terrific time together; there's more to what's written here. Overall, it was an overwhelming vacation, and we looked forward to more like it. We boarded our train to Mumbai and arrived in Goa early in the morning. Because the jet lag was getting to us, we napped at my parents' house in Mapusa before returning home that afternoon.

CHAPTER 4
HAPPY MOMENTS

PART II

After the great honeymoon vacation, we were happy all day; spending wild evenings recovering from the honeymoon hangover; we couldn't stop talking about our stay at Singapore and Malaysia. I was beaming, and so was Anay; our love was becoming stronger by the day, and we were doing it every day, sometimes twice. It was unstoppable.

One day, when we went for a drive, Anay received a call from the gang, the teenagers of his family visiting our residence and organizing a trip to Lonavala. We didn't want to go because we had recently returned from our honeymoon. We weren't interested in the idea, but his cousins wouldn't let up and pushed on us joining them; they insisted, saying *"it was my first vacation with the family, and so on... It will be enjoyable, etc."*, I was put up on an emotional trip, so we just gave in and began preparing for Lonavala.

CHAPTER 5
LONAVALA

Everyone was driving their own cars. We started early in the morning for Lonavala, matching the schedule of the others. It was my longest drive with Anay to Lonavala. I watched him drive the lovely Creta, and the music, halts, and sweet kisses along the route were beyond wonderful.

Anay's cousin had rented a bungalow from a friend for roughly three days. It was only going to be a brief journey. We arrived around 8 p.m. We were tired, so we ate and slept. The bungalow was well-appointed, with a swimming pool and a large "**Jhula**" on the porch. There were six rooms in all, and couples were given separate rooms while others mixed with whoever they pleased.

The bungalow's caretaker lady was lovely; she looked after us properly and was concerned about everyone's needs. She provided us with breakfast. Anay had bread and half-fried eggs with coffee while I had poha with chai. I remember it so well because he had told me that when we get home, he wanted this type of delectable breakfast every morning, to which I answered, *'kyun nahi'* with a wink and a half-smile on my face.

Day 1: We were in for a long day. We went to **Tungarli Dam** and **Lions Point**, and then we played games, etc. This time, we didn't take our separate cars. Instead, opted for 2 cars so that we could be together all the time and to have fun together because that was the plan; to have FUNNN along the trip.

Yayy!!!

We stopped for lunch and I overheard Anay's cousin saying, *'hope you are there tonight, let's have fun'* and I questioned, are you guys going to sit and drink all night? His cousin had brought bottles of beer and breezer. The plan was to stay awake all night, drink all night, and sit by the pool chit-chatting and, of course, playing games. It was then that I realized what they meant by games and more… This was the '**more**' element they were discussing. I didn't give Anay the typical wifey look. That's okay with me. I was like, I'll stay awake too. I won't drink beer but I can have a breezer, and I'm ready for games and laughter and for some gossip sessions.

We arrived at our bungalow after finishing our tour for the day. We changed into our jammies and got ready for some beverages and games. The crazy night we had planned began with Dumb Charades, Truth Or Dare, Spin The Bottle, Blindman's Swag, Passing the Parcel, and many more… Blindman's swag was my favorite of the bunch.

Anay is terrible at games; **(the only thing he excels at is mind games)**.

We were up all night, sitting by the pool and chit-chatting, cheering for drinks, making fun of each other, and having a good time. I was overjoyed to be growing closer to the family; knowing each of them made me feel alive and at ease. I was one of them now, and it felt great to have them around. Anay was overjoyed to see me bonding with everyone and having a good time. We called it a night soon.

Day 2: We were all set to visit **Shree Narayani Dham Temple** and **Amrutanjan Point**. We didn't do much. Overall, it was a great day.

Day 3 (LAST DAY): On the final day, we had planned to visit **Imagicaa**. It has a theme park, a water park, and a snow park. We went on several rides, experiencing each element of the adrenaline experience till late in the evening. We had supper out and returned home late that night. Everyone was having mixed feelings as the tour came to a close, and we were to return to our homes the next day.

I was lying on our bed with Anay, chatting about our good times, telling him how great I felt with all of them and how happy I was to be a member of this united family of such kind people. He smiled at me and embraced me, kissing my forehead, and we grew excited kissing each other. He then slid his hands inside my tee, sliding his fingers to my breast, as I closed my eyes, feeling his hand run over my body, slowly removing my tee, undressing himself, kissing my breasts... I moaned softly, tightening my grip on his hair, and guided him to kiss my stomach. I came over him, kissing his chest, my lips pressing against his body as he grabbed me and kissed my back, stripping me in every way, as we held our hands tight, and made love to one another.

We called it 'Lonavala Night'.

It had been emotional the next morning as we said our goodbyes and prepared to leave for home. We had a remarkable experience and the camaraderie we formed was remarkable as well. We took a family photo and then began our journey back home.

CHAPTER 6

HAPPY MOMENTS

PART III

A month and some days had passed by after returning from Lonavala when I began to feel dull and tired all day, unable to comprehend why I was feeling so agitated. In addition, I had skipped my periods. I was terrified of anything unexpected. I discussed the possibility of me being pregnant with Anay. He just brushed me off, assuring me that it wouldn't be that and that I was just weary of traveling so much. I was certain that I would have to face something for which I was unprepared. We did make love very regularly in between wiping off my worry.

The tiredness was becoming a little too heavy for me day by day. I eventually decided to have it examined. I told Anay to buy me a pregnancy test kit. I waited for a minute and it displayed "**Two Pink Lines**" indicating a positive result; I was astounded. I was hesitant to trust it. I wanted to be certain, so we made an appointment with our doctor right away. They took my urine and blood tests and said with a smile, "**You are Pregnant**," and inquired, "**Do you want to keep the baby?**"

In that room, with a knot in my throat, zillions of emotions were racing through my thoughts. I took a deep breath and asked the doctor if I may speak with my spouse. Anay was expecting me. I broke the news to him. He was thrilled as hell, while I was perplexed as hell. We didn't quarrel, but I asked him whether he had used condom properly or pulled out in time. I'm not sure if I was complaining, but I wanted time to comprehend this.

We took our time, but we needed to make a decision since every day of the week was crucial. The life inside of me was developing inch by inch, and Anay persuaded me to retain the baby because it was our first child and should not be aborted. He reassured me that we'd be okay and that the journey would be monumental. I gathered courage and chose to proceed with my pregnancy.

Though the thought of having a baby so early did cross my mind, I somehow believed that it would only add to the happiness in our world and there will be smiles along the way, bringing joy not only to us, but to the entire family, and the excitement of entering the phase of motherhood and becoming parents had me by the feet.

Nine months of pregnancy: First, Second, and Third Trimester.

Every time I saw my gynecologist, she would do sonography and show me how a baby the size of a little dot was floating in my womb. It gave me shivers, and I would express my excitement while waiting for the baby to begin its movements and kicks.

Because there is a significant chance of miscarriage during the first three months, my doctor advised me to relax as much as possible, avoid long distance travel, and keep a balanced diet. My first three months were rather trouble-free because I had no issues. I had my paperwork prepared for my doctor visits, so the appointments were pre-scheduled, and Anay never missed any appointment. He used to come to my check-ups and ask questions about my development. The doctor would add vitamins and tablets to my regimen to help my womb expand.

I was fine, and we used to go for short-drives, movies, and eat out. I had no idea how I had spent the first **five months** of this phase relaxing and having a good time.

I started feeling nauseated in the **sixth month**. I was craving a lot of Chinese and Vegetarian cuisine, but I was becoming grumpy all the time since my taste receptors were changing. I battled more, and Anay struggled to deal with my mood swings.

That month, our birthdays were approaching.

Anay's Birthday

I had prepared a celebration for Anay, and I also surprised him with a midnight cake. We snuggled up, and the next morning, on his birthday, we went to the temple for getting blessings before going out for lunch.

I had invited his friends, my parents, and his family members over in the evening. We cut the cake, and I gave him a watch as a present. He adored my present, and he adored me for throwing an extravagant party and making the occasion memorable.

My Birthday

Anay made my birthday memorable. We went out for lunch, where he ordered cake, brought me flowers, and gifted me a piece of jewelry. It was a gold ring with diamonds set in it. He knew the size of my finger as he took it when we were engaged. My joy knew no bounds; it was such a kind gesture. I wore it on my finger and showed it off. It was my first birthday with him after our marriage, and he had also organized a party at home in the evening, inviting my parents, his entire family, and some of his friends. I especially liked the cake he bought and the words written on it. It said: **"What makes me a great husband is having a great wife like you. I am nothing without you. Happy Birthday with all my love"**.

It was the nicest birthday I'd ever had.

My baby bulge began to appear around **7 months** and my baby shower was the only thing on everyone's mind. I was overjoyed, and Anay was as enthusiastic about planning everything for me, from the decorations to what I was going to wear, and so on… My check-ups were going well, and I had no issues.

I was all flowery, gaining weight, smiling, and thrilled to show off my baby bulge. I was sticking to my diet and taking all of the essential precautions to ensure a smooth delivery. The baby shower ceremony was limited to immediate family members and went quite well. I truly enjoyed it. We had some photos taken of Anay kissing my baby bulge and whispering in my ear whether he wanted a girl or a boy. It had been a day full of joy, happiness, and feelings. I was amazed by his family's affection, pampering, and care for me. I was making sure I didn't miss anything that came my way.

The 8th month was a tough one.

I experienced problems with gas, a lot of twisting and turning in bed, frequent urination, itching around the vaginal area, and unexpected cramps that scared me since I believed they were birth pains. But the nicest part was what I was looking forward to: my kid kicking me harder and moving around within my belly. I used to get emotional when I felt the baby kick and how the baby used to roll all day long; the baby's head could literally be seen like an imprint on my tummy. Both Anay and I used to leap with excitement experiencing all of that. I used to chat with my kid, asking to come out soon in my arms when the kicks were strong enough.

9th month

I was counting days.

The cramping became increasingly intense. The routine examinations had been shortened by a week, and I could now plainly see my baby floating in my womb in the sonography. I could hear the heartbeats and movements of its hands and legs. The doctor told me to count on 20 motions every day. That many counts are required because the water bag might burst anytime, leaving little space for the baby to move freely and eventually take position to come out.

I began counting, and at the start of the second week, I felt fewer motions. The count was not as expected, so I immediately phoned my doctor, who admitted me. Anay was tense. The doctor requested Anay to sign a permission form for our c-section birth. It was agreed between us that I would have a c-section. I wasn't prepared for regular labor pains, and the thought of normal delivery terrified me.

D-DAY

The doctor had told me to restrict eating anything substantial for eight hours before the C-section. I was asked to change into a gown before the nurse came to shave the pubic area and make the uterine incision across the lowest section of the uterus. We were waiting for the anesthesiologists to come so we could begin the procedure. He was there in around 15 minutes.

I went into the operating theater (also known as an operating room (OR). Everyone wished me a smooth delivery and a healthy baby. I started weeping because I was frightened to go through this. After administering anesthesia, the doctor calmed me down and advised me to lie down; he asked me which part of my body felt numb and heavy to lift. It was my legs and my entire tummy up to my breast. The OT lights turned on, and the doctor began the procedure. I didn't feel anything down there for approximately 30-45 minutes while my eyes were wide open. When I heard my baby's first cry, I burst into tears; those were happy tears, I was overjoyed. Finally, the procedure was through and the doctor began sewing me up.

I began to feel dizzy and fainted. The anesthesia had taken its toll on me. My eyes closed. I awoke about an hour later, with a mild headache and soreness in the upper quadrant of my belly. Then the nurse placed my baby in my hands. It was a boy. I clutched him in my hands. I felt an emotion I can't put into words. His small feet, tiny hands, and such a lovely and cute red face. His eyes were still shut, but his lips started moving as I softly kissed and touched him.

I was advised to breastfeed the baby. Because of its significance and hue, Colostrum is often known as "**liquid gold**". It has a high concentration of antioxidants and antibodies, which can help keep your infant healthy. Colostrum contains beneficial microorganisms that are needed for the lining in your baby's gut. It also includes chemicals that can nourish healthy bacteria while killing the bad ones. I nursed him. The nurse advised me to relax since the sutures were sore and needed to heal from the inside out.

I was in excruciating pain. As they say, parenthood is not easy. That is correct. I was in the hospital for about ten days.

Anay used to visit me, bring me food, and play with the newborn; it was then that I noticed that he was worried about something. I wondered what it might be. He wasn't really talking about it, and even though I asked him multiple times, he ignored me.

I was discharged from the hospital after healing from the sutures and finishing the necessary paperwork. Anay dropped me off at my parents' home in Mapusa for my post-delivery stay.

ONCE A MOTHER, ALWAYS A MOTHER… I was juggling a lot of things, such as my postpartum care, massages, nursing the baby every two hours, burping him, cleaning up the susu toilet. It was like being a ninja, rushing for my kid every time he wailed and soaked the bed. I couldn't devote much time to Anay, and we seldom communicated.

I was too occupied and the little time I had from my hectic routine of looking after the kid. I used to feel weary and dozed off in no time. Putting the infant to sleep and then getting up every two hours to nurse him was exhausting. It seemed like a 24-hour game.

CHAPTER 7

NAMING CEREMONY

On the 12th day came the naming ceremony; we had pre-determined the name; only I and Anay knew about it, and now was the day we were going to reveal it to everyone. **It was a moment of happiness.** The cradle decorations were on, and we just had the usual guests; not many people were invited because it was a closed occasion.

The function was scheduled to begin at 5 p.m. I was waiting for Anay to arrive; because I was preoccupied with my kid, I did not really check in on him to see what time he would be leaving, etc… I had told him last night that he needed to finish his work early that day and drive to Mapusa at the earliest after getting my jewelry for the event. (**Mistake No. 1: After our marriage, I gave Anay my gold jewelry in good faith for storing safely in his locker. I didn't have a locker in my name, which I should have done so that I could be accountable for my own belongings rather than relying on him**).

INSTANCE 1

It was 4 p.m., and Anay was nowhere to be seen. We kept trying to reach him on the phone, but he was always occupied. I began to worry. I was angry since I needed to get ready for the occasion and he had not arrived on time. I was irritated. Finally, he came at 5 p.m., forcing us to begin the event late. I was getting dressed while I questioned him why he was late and about my jewelry, he didn't respond. He hadn't brought my jewels with him.

I was surprised. I questioned as to why he hadn't brought them despite repeated reminders that I needed them for the function. Why didn't he bring them when he knew it was such an important occasion and I needed to wear them? I had a hunch that something was wrong. When I connected the dots, I recalled him being concerned about something in the hospital and ignoring me whenever I inquired about it. I had also asked him to hand my jewelry over to my parents for the naming ceremony function because they were visiting me in the hospital. I had thought I'd take the burden off Anay's head to get the jewels all the way to Mapusa, and to be on the safe side, I had insisted him to give it to my father whenever he visited me in the hospital, but Anay would refuse to do so, instead becoming furious and remarking that there was no need to wear them for the occasion because I'll be carrying the child, etc., and I was wondering why he was saying such strange things when all he could say was 'Okay, I'll grab it'.

I began to suspect that I had made a mistake by handing him my jewelry to be put in his locker and trusting him with them. But I had no proof, and he also would not have admitted that he had committed such an act. He threw in some evasive explanations for why he couldn't go to the bank and grab it from the locker. I shouted at him since he was plainly hurting me. I didn't have time to think about what was going on. The guests were waiting, so I postponed dealing with the matter and prepared myself, masking my injured emotions and carrying through the ceremony with a grin on my face.

We opened the slate after following the proper rites and named the newborn "**ABEER**". I had breastfed him well so that he didn't become irritable and cry. He slept through the entire ceremony. I didn't say anything to Anay during the ceremony. When the ceremony ended, I questioned him. His mother confessed that the jewelry had been mortgaged and that Anay did not have enough money to settle the interest on his business on a firm .opened

I was shocked upon hearing this because I had not consented to this mortgage and had no idea what was going on behind my back regarding his financial situation and problems. Anay had never discussed such matters with me. I burst into tears. It was too much for me. He didn't care about my sentiments and emotions. That was the first time I felt defeated by Anay. He had damaged my trust in him. How could he have done that? My mind began to race with all kinds of questions.

I urged him to leave; I needed time to comprehend what he had just done and cautioned him that I wanted my gold ornaments. Furthermore, I couldn't tolerate the lies he had told me that he couldn't go to the bank. He couldn't understand it even though I reminded him so many times. I couldn't truly digest it. He promised to return my jewelry in a few days.

Four Days Later...

He brought the jewelry. Again, I questioned him on how he had managed to obtain the mortgaged jewels in only four days, to which he answered that he had handled the finances somehow and avoided giving me the details. Somehow, I felt that he couldn't gather the guts to tell me the truth. I began to feel overwhelmed by his responses, so I phoned his mother, who admitted that he had redeemed mine by mortgaging her gold jewels, to which she had consented, to help Anay overcome his financial problems.

It was a catastrophe.

I confronted him. He said that he had suffered financial losses and that he would eventually make everything right, which was difficult to believe, but I was in such a state that I had no choice but to believe him. I couldn't tell my parents because I didn't want them to be stressed about it, and I needed to know what Anay was up to; I needed to protect him in some way, and I also needed to look after Abeer; it was too much for me to handle. I didn't know what to do.

I knew something wasn't quite right; I needed to investigate further, but I didn't know how… I simply believed Anay for the sake of believing him and begged him to restore his mother's jewelry. I couldn't stand the thought of my mother-in-law getting into trouble. I was worried about how she was feeling and what she was going through. It just increased my tension. While he was begging and apologizing for his actions, I wasn't completely persuaded, but because he was remorseful (**which he pretended to be**), I believed him and forgave him at that point of time.

Every relationship is built on the foundation of trust and requires time. Moreover, I am aware that no relationship, no matter how hard you try, is completely honest. There is a chance that one person will damage the other person's feelings, which is perfectly okay because we are all human and make errors; conflicts enhance love.

CHAPTER 8

HARSH REALITY - FLASHBACK

My father once said to me: there are two types of people in this world, the giver and the taker; the taker may eat better, but the giver always sleeps better.

It was time for me to return home, where I belonged. I was at a loss for words since my emotions were so heavy. It felt difficult, as if I didn't want to leave. It's weird after marriage, we women have to balance our sentiments of managing our parents' homes as well as our husband's homes, yet it's so lovely and safe for men that they never have to make those big changes in life like leaving their houses or making any major adjustments.

While Anay and I were traveling back home, all I could think about was returning to my parents. Something didn't feel right. I longed to see them; my heart felt incomplete . When I arrived home, we were greeted by firecrackers and balloons to celebrate the birth of Abeer and the routine of my 24-hour game with Abeer had begun. I also took the jewelry that Anay had brought back four days after the naming ceremony with me when I returned home. (Mistake No. 2: I should not have taken them back. I should have left them safe with my parents, knowing that Anay had broken my trust). I did not, however, give it to Anay to keep in his locker. Sometimes we take things for granted, believing that the person will not behave the same way after inflicting shame to the family hurting someone. We are so blinded by their love that we fail to see the storm approaching.

INSTANCE 2

Anay was quite secretive; I had no idea what he was up to; his attitude toward trivial issues bewildered me; he was behaving like an extremely typical male chauvinist pig. Whenever I asked him to help me with Abeer as I often got weary; his replies rattled me. He said that *'You are the mother. I won't help you with anything and as the mother, only you should be doing all of Abeer's duties'.* He would practically sleep when I stayed up late at night nursing Abeer and putting him to sleep, as if he didn't care or maybe he was so tensed up with something that he couldn't tell me openly. I began to feel down and sobbed beneath my pillow, missing my parents and having no one to share my feelings with. I couldn't even face his mother, knowing how upset she was over her jewels being mortgaged to protect mine. I was feeling bad about Anay's actions while Anay was just unconcerned about the situation. It was depressing.

I opened a conversation with Anay about his financial problems one night, asking him how he went down so much that he had to lie so much and mortgage jewelry like that. He never gave me a straight answer. Instead, he attempted to divert the conversation to something else. He didn't have a response, but his body language and actions made it evident that something was keeping him from opening up to me.

Several days passed. They weren't particularly good, they were normal, but something was brewing with Anay. I noticed the way he was throwing tantrums about everything; straining to express his point. His actions were erratic. He wasn't consistent with his everyday regimen. He gradually began to tell me that keeping the jewelry at home was risky. I requested him to buy me a locker in a bank, but he refused to obtain a locker, so I stored all of my jewelry in the locker in my closet.

(Here, the genuine narrative of Anay's manipulative mind games, emotional blackmailing, and fake promises begins, that things began to turn nasty and exacerbated following the lockdown in March; the beginning of the downfall of this relationship).

INSTANCE 3

Anay began whining about the state of his business and the financial concerns associated with it. He began receiving calls from the agents who were demanding money since he was not paying their dues on time. He informed me that one of his relatives was going to assist him in obtaining road building contracts, and that he required Rs. 7 lakhs to fill out the tender and then he would try to get his offer approved to build the road. He began to put pressure on me to assist him with the initial amount to be given as a token.

I initially refused to assist, telling him that the business difficulties were his fault and that he should not involve me in them.

He would refuse to listen and emotionally blackmail me into assisting him in overcoming his business losses and challenges.

He told me that if I didn't ask my father for money or help him with his funds to cover his business losses, he would commit suicide. He'd then ask me, *"What is more important to you, your husband or your money?"* I started to get very depressed over such statements and such blackmail tactics used by him. After persistent pressure from him, I gave him some of my gold ornaments as I didn't want to drag my father into this mess. Anay promised to return my ornaments by the end of the month. He never returned them. **(Mistake No. 3: Trust and vulnerability are intertwined. I gave myself permission to be open and susceptible; the simplest act of trusting someone to keep their word exposes you to the risk of betrayal.**

I should not have lent my jewelry to Anay to assist in safeguarding the so-called difficulties sweet-talked by him, without first obtaining permission from my parents or his parents, believing that I was defending my spouse and hoping that my sentiments and emotions would soon not be taken for granted. Clearly, I was not strong enough to take the necessary action, thus, I invited problems into my life.

I started growing scared about the whole affair. I knew I'd made the worst mistake of my life by believing in his phony tears and assisting him with the road contract nonsense. I had taken a great risk by lending him my jewels without informing anybody at home, not even my parents. I was beginning to feel like an emotional idiot and felt that I had gotten myself into a tremendous issue while Anay was trying my patience. I used to beg Anay to return my jewelry, which he had promised to return, but he just ignored the problem and we started fighting over the issue that he didn't have enough money to redeem them. I couldn't tolerate it. My mental and physical health as well as my emotional condition began to worsen, and I was not able to properly focus on Abeer. My focus had become unsteady.

I was tense. I had difficulty dealing with Anay's mind games and falsehoods. I began bursting out on him; our fights used to bother his parents, and when they found out, he began assaulting me and cursing me behind closed doors, for bringing the fight out openly in front of his parents. He was also threatening them to not get involved in any of our matters and to stay away from our fights; I used to be terrified by his actions; it was cynical.

My tears used to dry when I saw Anay raise his hand on me, smack me, rip my hair, and toss me on the bed. I didn't seek any aid and wept for hours. After a while, he would come to me and apologize for his acts, saying that were unintentional, but even if I did forgive him, understanding his plight, it would leave a permanent scar on my heart about his uncontrollable anger. The treatment he gave me, even after I assisted him in his rough patch, plainly proved that he was not responsible for his actions and that he was inhuman.

I stayed silent, tolerating abuse since my mind was racing with a million concerns about how I was going to tell my parents about it. What if something were to happen to them? Who should I approach, and what should I do? What about Abeer? How am I going to get out of this mess? I used to feel burdened by this connection, so I prayed and hoped for relief, answers, and miracles. I really needed a miracle in my life. Anay's continuous assaults and animal-like conduct had depleted me.

Things started getting ugly as fuck. We didn't communicate much, and when we did, it was mainly about his problems. Something was tearing me apart. I gave Anay numerous chances to help return things to normalcy. I tried to soothe his situation in every way, trying hard to understand what he might be going through, but with his repulsive behavior, he always ended up pushing me away from him and reverting to his criminal attitude.

Trust had plummeted, fissures had appeared, and there was no love, intimacy, or understanding in this relationship. I became depressed and wept my heart out, sobbing endlessly. I longed for a solution. I hated myself for putting up with him at festivals and family functions, pretending we had a strong bond in front of his family. In a shared family setting, I pretended to be okay, covering my suffering, concealing everything by feigning a smile with a heavy heart. I was dealing with anxiety and tension, looking for methods to fix this despite all the odds he had put me through, with a single ray of hope that one day, everything would be okay.

INSTANCE 4

Anay owed money to a number of people. One day, a gentleman came to our house to recover his money. Anay kept making false promises to him. He arrived at the house one day and refused to go until he was paid. Then Anay used blackmail techniques on me, threatening that if I did not give him my remaining ornaments to mortgage them, he would perhaps face legal action. I was horrified to see these things happening. Anay was in so much debt that people began coming to our home to retrieve their money; I was pained to watch Anay's financial blunders and how his behaviors were impacting me, putting me in a lot of difficulties. (**Mistake No. 4: I should not have considered the legal implications Anay would face. I was again being emotional and making decisions to lend him my remaining jewels; instead, I should have phoned my father and confronted him immediately to avoid more complications**).

Anay was using my emotional weakness by displaying his fragility and playing with my emotions. To avoid further humiliation of the family, I offered him my remaining ornaments to mortgage in order for him to raise some money and repay the gentleman.

I was caught up in a cycle of grief, tension, and whatnot. I had absolutely lost it, but I was still hoping it would all come to an end eventually. I was having trouble figuring out how to get out of this situation. I had made a major mistake by not including my parents in this entire situation right from the start. I was hurt in every way, physically plunging into problems one after the other while floating on the surface.

Anay didn't appreciate my efforts to right things; he wouldn't even let me go to my parents' place for the fear that I would spill the beans and he would have to face the consequences; he feared the consequences, but made no efforts to change his condition. Additionally, when questioned on the same. I received the unexpected. Anay assaulted me and broke all of his fraudulent promises.

INSTANCE 5

Anay persuaded my father to lend him Rs. 5 lakhs under the guise of requiring cash for his business. My father was completely unaware that Anay had mortgaged my valuables. My father offered him Rs. 3 lakhs as a token of assistance to his son-in-law. My father called and informed me of the situation. I was saddened to hear this, but I couldn't show my father how far I had fallen. Anay said that he needed the money to purchase inventory for his store. It resulted in another argument, first over my jewelry, and then over this. I was stressed, wondering about how he would return my father's money.

I'd had it with Anay. All of my efforts and sacrifices were in vain.

Needless to say, Anay did not manage to return this sum to my father. Things were slipping out of hand uncontrollably. I was scared because I could see a valley that was so steep that I couldn't figure out where it was leading me or where it was going to end.

INSTANCE 6

An elderly gentleman, who had fallen prey to Anay's sweet talk and had given him Rs. 2 lakhs, began visiting our home, and each time he arrived, Anay would take him into our bedroom and have lengthy conversations with him. I was completely unaware of what was going on. One morning, after the elderly gentleman left our house, I confronted Anay in front of his mother and asked him why that person came over to our house every day.

Anay told me, in the presence of his mother, that he had taken Rs. 2 lakhs from him and that he was now asking him to pay up, or else he would file a police complaint, commit suicide, and blame Anay for his death. I was like FUCK! Even his mother was horrified and began crying in despair when she heard it, and my situation was no different. I yelled at Anay for always putting me and his family in danger; why and how could he be so inhuman and inconsiderate that he never valued our feelings? My mother-in-law was equally stressed because Anay still hadn't returned her mortgaged jewels; how could Anay forget all of that and be so inhuman, making us go through this torture? It was completely unacceptable and unjustifiable.

Anay begged me once again to save him because he was afraid of the repercussions of borrowing money from that man.

Anay couldn't manage the pressure the old gentleman had put on him. I didn't understand what the heck was going on. It felt as if I was a multitude of fixes to every goddamn problem. It had put up with enough. My mother-in-law had witnessed this incident. She was worried and upset. She felt helpless. To avoid being backed into a corner by the emotional blackmail, I decided to assist Anay with the savings I had, not for Anay's sake, but for that elderly man and my mother-in-law, in order to keep him from experiencing unforeseen problems he might face if that elderly man committed suicide owing to Anay's failure to pay his money.

Anay assured me that he would return my money; however, he never did, and I never asked him to. To some extent, I had lost confidence and trust in him; he had tormented me to the point where I could no longer believe him. I finally decided to take a stand for myself because I could no longer tolerate his behavior, so I stated loudly and clearly in front of his parents that if Anay continued this behavior, I would leave him and this house and take appropriate legal action against Anay, and that solutions to his problems should come from his family and his parents without putting me in further trouble. Enough now.

I wanted to put an end to everything, and I hoped that my warning would make Anay recognize his mistakes. I waited, hoping that Anay would see my value, my sentiments, emotions, and love for him. Nevertheless, time and truth always meet. The question is not about who is correct or incorrect, but what is correct or incorrect. I accept full responsibility for the mistakes I made.

Over Trust, Over-Care, and Over-Love

I ran out of my savings, my jewelry was mortgaged, and I had nothing left with me; I was literally trying everything to fix things, but I was drifting apart from Anay as he never understood my concerns for him and the seriousness of how badly I wanted him to rectify his mistakes and be a better person for once. I longed for him to amend his ways. I wanted him to be truthful; transparent to me, discuss with me, and respect me for god's sake, but he wouldn't listen. He never realized how serious that was. I was frustrated. It formed a rift, a substantial split between us.

Anay promised to pay off the mortgage and return my gold within six months. After the end of the said period, when I began asking him to return my gold ornaments, he kept assuring me every day; making false promises that he would redeem the mortgage as well as return my money, which never happened, but what did happen was that we were living a relationship with no trust and no meaning left. It had devolved into hollow with no regard for one another. It was a struggle to survive.

My instincts were screaming at me that something bad was about to happen. All along the said period and beyond that, I had undergone immense mental torture; the torture had started affecting my health. I had attempted in good faith to help Anay and prevent him from doing anything wrong with his life for the sake of our marriage and our son. Anay never tried enough to explain the proper issue or tell me the truth. His actions became increasingly questionable as time passed.

Whenever I inquired about my gold or how he intended to pay the money he had borrowed from my father, he became aggressive he would physically assault me, emotionally blackmail me, and put me under immense mental stress.

INSTANCE 7

The Chaturthi festival was approaching, and Anay and I were to execute a ritual called "Houso". I was begging Anay to find a way to retrieve my gold jewelry, warning him that if he fails to do so, I would not attend the ritual. Since he had mortgaged all of my jewelry and we were arguing day and night over it, I was terrified that something unexpected or upsetting was in store for me.

To my surprise, Anay was able to obtain my jewelry for the ritual. I was astounded to see my jewelry after such a long time. I asked him how he managed to release the gold. Since he was facing financial difficulties and was in debt, there was no way he could redeem the gold; I even asked him whether he had released his mother's jewels as well. He referenced obtaining support from his political contacts as he was active in local politics, and that the money owed to them would be taken care of. He told me that all of his financial problems had been resolved and that I had assisted him in getting through them; he also mentioned about paying my father's money and mine too. **(Mistake No. 5: I should not have believed him so quickly; whatever he stated about arranging money through some political links should have been double-checked or investigated to see whether he was telling the truth. I was so taken with my jewelry that I didn't try to inquire any farther, trusting his fabricated lies).**

I was happy. I thought, okay, fine, maybe helping Anay was worth it all. Bad patches do come, and all of this happened because of such unfortunate circumstances. I believed this was the end of my sufferings, and the start of a beautiful life with Anay that I didn't see it coming. I immediately began to believe that I had not been mistaken in trusting Anay and that he had also faced a lot in all these matters. It was a tough time for both of us; now he had gotten my jewelry, although a few items were missing, he admitted that he couldn't manage it all, and he did not succeed in redeeming his mother's jewels, which was upsetting, but he stated that he would gradually try to redeem them.

People often fail to perceive the flaws of someone they love. In this situation, the proverb **"love is blind"** was most suited to me.

I wore the jewelry at the "Houso" ritual and then retained it with me.

INSTANCE 8

My younger brother was to marry. I was overjoyed to be the Karavali - a term for the bride's or bridegroom's sister (or female officiating). I had big plans for shopping, functions, etc. Everything appeared to be in order until a few days later, when Anay charmed me and assured me that as a token of thanks, he wanted to surprise me with a gold ornament. He also requested that I give over all of the gold ornaments to him so that he may have them cleaned by a jeweler before my brother's wedding.

(Mistake No. 6: I should not have trusted his assurances and been such a fool in lending him what I had acquired after so many problems, tension, and suffering).

I gave Anay the jewelry to be polished.

Not to pay the mortgage. I didn't even know his intention behind taking it. Anay cheated me, claiming it was for polishing, and later mortgaged it WITHOUT MY CONSENT. He clearly knew I wouldn't consent to any extra assistance with the jewelry mortgage, so he opted to

defraud me, something I was plainly ignorant of, since I had assumed he had taken the jewelry for cleaning.

Before my brother's wedding, I kept reminding Anay to bring my gold jewels back from the jeweler, but he continued making false promises. I was back in the same drill of pain, feeling defeated, and begging Anay to return my jewelry.

He indicated to me, albeit falsely, that he would surprise me by giving me additional gold ornaments when he would bring my old gold ornaments and that I need not be concerned since I would have all of my gold ornaments in time for the wedding and the other functions before and after the marriage. The last time I knew he had mortgaged them, but this time I had no idea what he had done because whenever I asked, he denied that he mortgaged them, instead assuring me that the polishing work had not been completed, and that the new jewelry was still in process.

I couldn't believe it. I loathed myself for believing him. The suspense was killing me. He kept insisting that he hadn't mortgaged them... and polishing wouldn't take this long, then where did the jewels go? Our arguments were getting uglier by the day, with striking going both ways and assaults increasing. I was scared. I was stunned; what would I tell my parents now? How would they respond if Anay fails to bring the jewels in time for the wedding?

He continued postponing the date to return my jewelry until the day I departed for Goa. I had a hunch that something was dreadfully wrong. My brother's wedding was approaching, and I didn't have much time. I was in a lot of trouble, wondering how I was going to deal with everything. On the day before my intended departure for Goa, I insisted on receiving my gold jewelry, which angered him to the point of assaulting me.

I had a separate wardrobe with a locker, where I kept my personal belongings, and some valuables belonging to me and our son. Anay had accessed my wardrobe locker without my permission. Before leaving for Goa to stay with my parents in preparation for my brother's wedding, I opened my wardrobe locker to grab gold chains that had been gifted to our son so that I could make him wear them at the wedding functions. When I couldn't locate them in the locker, I inquired Anay about it. He admitted to taking it, but was ambiguous about whether he had pawned it to make money or not. I rebuked him for opening my wardrobe without my consent and taking my things from it to which he replied that he has an equal right to take whatever he wants as Abeer is his son too.

Such an act was an affront on my privacy and against my right to have exclusive ownership of my personal items. But, to avoid creating an issue at the time of leaving the house, I asked Anay to bring them along with my gold jewelry when he would come for the wedding ceremonies of my brother. He dropped me off in Goa. **(Redirecting to Chapter 1- The Black Day to allow readers to connect the dots).**

CHAPTER 9

DISPUTE

"A man is great by deeds, not by birth".

- Chanakya

Spending 2 years, 11 months, and 6 days with Anay and countless days without him, I can't explain, but each day that went by felt like a decade, thinking, "Why me?" My heart and intellect were fighting each other, searching for solutions. Loyalty is never murky. It is in monochrome. Either you are wholly faithful or you are not. Anay was neither trustworthy nor dependable. Sometimes your heart takes more time to embrace what your head already understands.

The most tough and demanding period of my life, the myriad days and months I wish I could delete. The difficult days when everything seemed unattainable made me cry, days when I cried in the shower; days when I sobbed under my pillow; days when I yelled in my space; days when I was frustrated and angry; days when I wanted to shout out loud without being heard; days when I wanted to sleep, sleep, sleep, and not wake up; days when I stared at the ceiling without blinking; Days when a tear rolled down my cheek and I quickly wiped it away to hide it from my mother, and days when she knew I was crying all night, looking at my puffy eyes in the morning, hugging me; taking away my pain, worries, and tension; making me feel like a baby in her womb; so light, so free, floating like a bubble, sucking only love and concern.

I felt the saddest about concealing everything about Anay from my mother. I was strong on most days. Some days, I was so angry with Anay that the thought of ever forgiving him seemed absurd; on other days, I missed him so badly. I miss the good old days spent with him, the laughter we had. I was missing making love to him. It literally ripped me apart.

I'd fought till this point to be strong, to not feel sorry for myself around other people. But I couldn't hide my feelings from my mother. I desired vulnerability. I just wanted to give up for a short bit. I wanted her to take over and hug me and assure me that everything will be okay. And when I cried in her arms, I just stopped fighting for myself, because I needed someone else to do it for me. I told her about most of the key aspects about our relationship, saying he had assaulted me on several occasions, and that I was afraid and didn't know what to do. I was afraid of being too frail and sensitive. Basically, I told her everything that I hadn't been courageous enough to acknowledge to myself.

My mother asked: "Would you like to take him back?"
I didn't say yes, but I didn't say no too.

That was the first time I'd been entirely honest ever since this happened. I was truthful to both her and myself, perhaps because she is the only person intimately familiar with my heart. She is the only one who can comprehend my state of mind. I told her that I would never trust him again. However, a large part of me missed what I had with him. We were good together, Mom. The times I spent with him were among the most memorable of my life. And sometimes I feel like I don't want to give that up.

I absolutely get what you're saying. However, you have to be strong enough to understand your limits.

Everything has a limit. There's a limit to what we're willing to tolerate before we snap. When Anay struck you for the first time, he apologized instantly and promised he would never do it again. Then, gradually.... with each occurrence, it increased... It persisted because you allowed it to happen by stretching your own boundaries, and he began to regard you as helpless, taking you for granted, thinking that his conduct was okay.

Don't let that happen, Meera; I know you believe he loves you, but he's not loving you properly. He doesn't love you the way you deserve. If he genuinely loves you, let him show you through his actions that he realizes that whatever he did was wrong and that he would make things right in order to regain your trust and forgiveness. Check on his efforts to reclaim you, and you will find out".

She held me tightly. She was completely correct in her assessment of what I deserved to be and what my position should be. She's one of the strongest women. She cheered me up, assuring me not to worry about anything since she is WITH me, FOR me, and BESIDES me. She took my hand in hers and told me that she was proud of me, and exclaimed, "*BE BRAVE!*' a tear escaped from her eye.

"It's okay to cry when there's too much on your mind - the clouds rain too when things get heavy". - Amina Mehmood

I gathered myself, brushing my tears away in thin air, and assured myself that I am a strong woman. I do not want to wallow in self-pity or appeal to others' compassion. I do not want to react to the negativity that surrounds me; or to those who tell me to accept reality as it is. However, I hoped for a little chance that Anay might change for the better, and I kept an eye out for his damage-control attempts. I wanted to fight even harder because I am a survivor, not a victim. I am in command of my life, and there is nothing I cannot accomplish.

My strength comes from being put to the test by the unpredictability of life. That which does not kill us strengthens us. I continued to take courage as the greatest defense because a woman is unstoppable after she realizes that she deserves better. I do not deserve to have my neck strangled. I do not deserve to be slapped. I do not deserve to be smacked against the wall, and certainly not getting booted for being present through thick and thin.

Self-respect and violence "**CAN-NOT**" coexist. You cannot heal in the same place where you got sick. I take satisfaction in having chosen my battle intelligently against a man who needed to understand a woman's vitality. I simply knew that I had to confront the cruel truth and reality with optimism and a smile. Goodbyes don't hurt as much as the flashbacks of memories that follow.

But the good news is... it can only get better from here.

I filed a Domestic Violence complaint against Anay for mortgaging my streedhan without my consent and hitting me, among other things, for lying to me about things that otherwise requires transparency between a husband and wife, and for causing me mental pain.

Teach your heart to accept loss and disappointment, even from those you care about.

CHAPTER 10

MEDIATION PROCESS
- 60 Days

"There is no such thing as bad people. We are all just people who do bad things".

- Colleen Hoover

It had been five months since the lawsuit was filed, and those months had been difficult, with much patience and anguish spent attending the hearing and facing Anay as the defendant. I only wanted Anay to value my worth and prove his love for me by correcting his behavioral patterns; I was hurt to witness the kind of attitude he displayed in court, becoming aggressive toward me for filing a case against him, not understanding why I had done that and that he was responsible for putting me in this situation.

While the dispute was ongoing, what hurt me more than the actions I was taking against Anay was having Anay in the courtroom as my defense. Not in my wildest fantasies had I imagined that we'd be in this situation. But that was necessary because I could no longer take his attitude toward the entire affair. It was deepening my melancholy even further. I had complete trust that my efforts would result in something positive for us, but Anay's actions proved me incorrect at every level of the conflict, harming my emotions and ruining my love. He was actually bringing me to the point where I lost my calm and lost hope of things getting better between us.

His behavior was driving me to the stage where I would give up on him and prepare myself to leave him and file for divorce. I was desperate for him to make things right for me and restore my trust in him. That was exactly what I desired from him. I craved his affection and wanted him to make the right choices. I yearned for him. I missed him, and even though I barred him from my call list, I couldn't block him from my heart, and whenever I unblocked him from my call list, we ended up bickering and going through the same drill.

I was encouraging him to understand that I wanted him to win my trust through his deeds rather than his words. I wanted him to be honest with me and protect my self-esteem. He was sorry, he had said it many times, he explained many times that his intention was not to hurt me or break my trust, but circumstances had forced him to do so, he kept lying to me and hiding things from me with the fear of losing me and fear of how I would react. He feared the circumstances and kept putting things aside, making a heap of lies that became intolerable, unbearable, and unacceptable. I was no longer in a position to trust him since my heart just did not accept what he was saying as I had already gone through enough of it. He was begging me to believe him just one more time, but I was not ready to trust him.

I was struggling with my emotions while comprehending what Anay was attempting to accomplish; he knew how to give me an emotional trip since he knew I was weak in that area, and I was perplexed as to whether I should trust Anay or not. I considered giving it a chance as a trigger to know what he was up to when he apologised, explaining that his actions were unintentional, and what circumstances forced him to lie and behave the way he did.I wanted to double-check his actions. So I presented the case for settlement, showing my trust in Anay, which led him to surrender my gold jewelry, which he had mortgaged, and as a result, the court transferred our matter from dispute to mediation. The court directed us one month to mend our damaged relationship and resolve our differences. I considered giving it a go to see how it turned out. I was going to see Anay again at his place.

It was the most difficult decision for me since no one agreed with the step I had taken; it carried a great deal of risk because believing Anay was still not convincing to my heart; my heart was roaring in denial, but I wanted to take a chance of delving deep into what he had made me believe. The mediation had begun in the first week of August, and the Ganesh Chaturthi festival was approaching, so I decided to rejoin Anay on Rakshabandhan.. A day before departing at his place. Because I was uncertain about him and I wanted to probe deeper. My brother texted me, asking for Anay's Aadhar card in order to learn more about his financial irregularities. The next morning, my brother checked Anay's Aadhar card, which was linked to CIBIL, and Woahhh!!!!

An unexpected BOMB blasted on me.

Chances are granted to those who earn them, and mistakes are forgiven if the courage to recognize them is there. What you do after you've made your errors makes all the difference. Mistakes do not make you less competent. Lingering in the past does nothing; God uses it to purify us; he predicts failures and plans ahead only to make us stronger, more like him, and more reflective of him. Anay was not guilty; he had the audacity to use emotions as a tool to his benefit, which he did; but what he miscalculated was that a woman becomes dangerous when she understands that her value does not depend on what her spouse or others acknowledge.

I had tied my worth to the nonsense he had made me believe. **CIBIL (the credit information bureau (India) limited)** was crucial in helping me comprehend how deep the cut was, i.e., it helped me in determining Anay's goals and games. I'd like to thank my brother for assisting me in obtaining the facts and serving as an eye-opener. One of the nicest presents he could offer me on 'Raksha Bandhan' was to save me from heading towards that deathtrap.

I modified the GAME by hurling a bomb at him at full speed, which killed him from within and made him wonder "HOW???" when I confronted him about the CIBIL report. Everything he had mentioned about secured and unsecured loans, obligations, and mortgages before and after the marriage had me gasping and fainting; the statistics had me panting; the shock of having me comprehend how fraudulent one can become. He responded, and not to my surprise,

VIOLENTLY. OBJECTIVE ACHIEVED.

What can a coward do for himself in such a haste?

He took advantage of the circumstance and took Abeer. Abeer had been with me for the past eight months since the time I arrived for my brother's wedding; it was not easy for me while I was going through the phase of dispute and handling Abeer; it takes a lot of courage to stand strong when all you want to do is to give everything up, let time stop, like a magic wand, taking away all the problems, making everything happy-go-lucky. It was a festive period, and I assumed Anay would bring him back after the Ganesh Chathurti celebrations since I couldn't stop him from having Abeer because he was Abeer's father, and I didn't want Abeer to suffer as a result of our conflict.

Our next hearing came by, settlement was rejected as inquiries involving newly discovered information about secured and unsecured loans, debts, and mortgages before and after marriage, etc. were submitted through CIBIL additionally, on not bringing Abeer back; withholding him, causing me deep agony. When I filed the DV, it was apparent that my kid was and should be in my custody, Anay was only permitted to have him for a limited period of time since he was his father; he was supposed to return him to me after that period, but what can I expect from a man like Anay, who never kept his word? This is how Anay plays games; filthy politics using Abeer as his pawn to damage me and cause me anguish.

The court issued an order, allowing me to visit the matrimonial home within a specific time frame in order for me to meet my son as well as directing the return of my belongings because I had come to Goa for a set period of time for my brother's wedding, not knowing I would ever have to go through this. I had brought only a few clothes and other documents that were equally important for me to bring in order for me to make further decisions on my career as I needed to be financially independent to raise Abeer. When I reached Anay's house, I was expecting to see Abeer, but he was nowhere to be seen; I asked Anay about Abeer's whereabouts, to which he responded that Abeer had gone to the park. I asked him why he had sent him when he knew I was coming, It was obvious that he had planned it, barring me from meeting Abeer; I stayed quiet since I didn't want to cause a fuss over there as ordered by the court; I discreetly began packing my belongings as I had only a certain time period to do it.

While packing my belongings, memories flashed through my mind as I observed the room I lived in for the years I spent with Anay. The good, bad, and worse days in that room gave me shivers. I realized how far I had come in my struggle. In that room, I built a home for the life I dreamt with Anay. I was feeling empty as I packed my things and left the place where I had been welcomed with tremendous love. I was feeling all of those sentiments when I got married and came into that home as I descended down the stairwell and left his home, not knowing where this was leading me.

I had trouble dealing with the heavy sensations I felt deep within after returning from Anay's place. I became insomniac, thinking about how Anay had behaved, forbidding me from meeting Abeer while I was so considerate when he took Abeer with him, thinking he has equal rights on Abeer, but Anay never thought the same way. He was depriving me of Abeer. I couldn't bear the thought of not having Abeer with me.

I realized I was striving to be the best version of myself for Anay, who had always been the wrong man for me. Not having Abeer with me made me unresponsive to Anay.

The 60-day mediation period was coming to a close, but Anay didn't stop playing. He skipped on every hearing with false excuses since he didn't want to give Abeer back to me. When the judge noticed his behavior, disobeying the court's repeated orders to return Abeer, the court reported our mediation as a failure and moved our matter back to dispute. Anay seemed unconcerned about what was going on and showed no remorse; he simply wanted me to forget everything and rejoin him without attempting to regain my self-esteem. He was apologizing with no intention to change his behavior. Thus, I believed I should prevent my heart from trusting him. I blocked his calls from then on, despite the misery I was in, wondering why he always hurt me and messed with my emotions. No matter how many times he tried to reach me or begged me to return, trying to make me understand that he was sorry, not making any effort to bring Abeer to me was clearly portraying that his mindset hadn't changed. I didn't believe anything he said. There was just one thought on my mind: I would not return to him. I was not allowing him to speak to me. I was entirely encased in my cocoon, refusing to let him in.

You are always **ONE DECISION AWAY** from living a completely different life.

Relationships develop when two people desire to grow together; I wanted to grow, no matter what it took, even if it meant growing without Anay; I reminded myself, "I **am ENOUGH for Myself**." The worst battle I have ever fought was between what I knew and what I felt.

CHAPTER 11

WITHOUT ABEER - (PART 1)

"You fall, get up, make mistakes, learn from them, be human and be you"

- Priyanka Chopra Jonas

My heart feels heavy. I feel a lump in my throat as I write this section, tears streaming down my cheeks; sinking in deep; finding words, what do I write in here? It was difficult for me to cope with the pain of being separated from my child, especially since I had legal custody of Abeer and Anay had taken it away from me.. Can a mother be challenged how she manages to stay away from her kid, especially when snatched from her forcibly? Anay' was taking advantage of the situation by taking Abeer away from me to cause me grief, suffering, and torture. It was indeed a challenge, but that's not what I felt awful about. Even though it was a cheap game; the most difficult aspect was living without Abeer, thinking how my days would be spent without him

A hole formed in my heart; I felt emptiness, aching for him with each passing day. I missed having him by my side as he woke up after cuddling him cutely in the night, his good morning kisses, feeding him food, bathing him, and playing with him… putting him to sleep in the afternoon; holding and caressing him, and the way he woke up cranky in the evening, asking me to go to the garden to play on the slider. He loved playing on the slider and the see-saw and then he used to run away from me, asking me to catch him. I wanted to go back to all of that; it was so cute, but Anay had made it impossible for me to reach my son.

How could somebody be so cruel?

Yes, the nights were tough; I missed telling Abeer all timepass bedtime stories… His innocent eyes; the way he used to gaze at me, paying attention; his wandering eyes were damn affectionate and I loved the way he used to sleep while holding me, with his head on my lap.

I was missing Abeer like crazy. It was starting to affect my health. I became sad and moody over petty things. I was losing everything. The worst part was continually thinking about how Anay had refused to let me meet Abeer and refused to agree to return him even after I told him that it was unfair to use that tiny baby as a pawn to cause me agony.

I was exhausted and needed to do something to occupy myself. I listened to music, which helped, but not significantly. I began reading books to keep myself occupied… Insomnia had taken over. I binge-watched Netflix to divert my attention, until I met Naresh. I give him complete credit. Naresh was driving us (myself, my mother, and my aunt) to Cumbarjua to give some items over to one of our relatives. I asked him, *"Will you teach me how to drive?"* He immediately agreed, and I began my classes with him every evening for approximately 2 hours, Perfect Timing.

Driving gave me a sense of independence, freedom, and soothed my feelings. I enjoyed learning. It made me feel good about myself. I truly loved setting aside those two hours as "**Me Time**". It did help me develop a little. Being apart from Abeer was more stressful than coping with Anay and his actions. It was shattering me. One day, when I was seated on my living room couch. My mother was a huge help to me throughout this time. It wasn't easy for her too, but I didn't grasp her sentiments since I was so caught up in my own thoughts that I couldn't understand what she was trying to say. She came over and sat next to me. Her words were comforting enough.

*"I understand what you're going through, "*she said.

"I completely get how you feel". I am also a mother, but I don't want you to let go of this period of sobbing and holding up.

Anay has already squandered your years by not allowing you to achieve anything positive, and now he's doing it again by stalling Abeer… Couldn't you see it coming? There are things that are important and vital for your growth and future. She meant my professional development.

You have to start from scratch, and I will always be there for you, no matter what… To gain something, you have to do something, not lose something, she explained. *Take your time, but consider it not for anybody else, but for yourself and Abeer in the long run,* she concluded.

Yeah, yes, yes!! I honestly did not see that coming. That's when it struck me, and it hit me really hard. While Abeer was away, I thought that I should use this opportunity to focus on myself and choose a career path that will enable me to improve in many aspects of my life. It truly educated me. I opened my diary; I have a practice of recording my interests and wishlist on a dairy; I make it a point to write everything down. It aids me in understanding my thought process. In it, I had mentioned that I enjoy HRM(Human Resource Management). I gave it a lot of thought before deciding. I realized what I wanted to do with my career and decided to shape my future accordingly. I took a leap of faith and allowed myself enough space to understand a pathway that opened new possibilities for me. I boosted myself by embarking on a new chapter.

I inquired about numerous HR training programmes. I came across **Metier HR Services** and contacted them. I spoke with **Mr. Milan Surana, HR Trainee & Motivational Speaker,** inquiring about the course, duration, and pricing structure. Mr. Surana explained everything to me and provided me with the Brochure and Enrollment form to fill out.

I waited a month to decide whether it was the right path for me since I was dealing with trust issues and all the difficult situations, so I took my time going forward with it. I wanted to be sure, so after going through the brochures and everything, I made up my mind and thought of visiting Pune to have a direct one-on-one conversation with Mr. Surana and get myself assured of the course's information and authenticity.

CHAPTER 12

PUNE CALLING

"Actions speak louder than words".

Difficult roads often lead to beautiful destinations.

I had my trip tickets booked with Indigo Airlines and was ready to embark on a solo journey to discover myself. It had been three long years since I had flown; I had lost touch with the airport; as soon as I arrived at the airport, I felt as if I had inhaled the oxygen I craved. The spirit of performing something was already making me feel light and had me kicking.

I landed in Pune in an hour. My brother had come to receive me at the airport, and because it was a late night flight, we didn't talk much. He left for work the next morning while I was left to figure out why I had come. I called Mr. Surana and scheduled my meeting; in the meantime, I went to Tulsi Baug and picked up some items and decorative pieces that my mother had instructed me to get, as well as taking darshans of **Shreemant Dagdusheth Halwai Ganpati**. After that, I went to meet Mr. Surana at the agreed time.

I was happy to visit Pune. I felt warm, especially because of Milan Surana, one of the most soft-spoken, humble professionals I've ever met. He promised to help me in building my core in HR profession, giving me the confidence to start from scratch. Thank you very much. And that's how Pune happened. I felt motivated after the meeting and I knew that I wanted to achieve this. I told my brother about the course and my level of interest, and he encouraged me to pursue my professional goals. I didn't stay there for long because it was a short trip, and I had my flight arranged for my return back to the pavilion with tremendous satisfaction of steering myself into a vision of reconstructing myself.

CHAPTER 13

WITHOUT ABEER - (PART 2)

"Life just keeps moving. You have to keep your blinkers on. Find what you do best and keep moving.

- Priyanka Chopra Jonas

After having returned from Pune, I was certain that I wanted to begin the HRM course with Metier HR Services. I registered in order to pursue a career in Human Resources.

Putting my blinkers ON, I was trying hard not to let my focus get wobbly and distracted by the feelings that were making me weak within the heart, battling the hollowness of missing Abeer while studying the course I had planned to take. The sessions were planned for two days a week, with homework in between. Mr. Milan Surana was an excellent trainer. I became engrossed in learning and studying, with just one objective in mind: I need to accomplish this in the near future, not only for myself, but also for Abeer.

There were days when I felt extremely frustrated, thinking about Abeer, missing him, and longing for him, but all I could do was pray to Ganesha to keep him happy, safe, and cheery at all times. Carrying this emotional baggage within me pushed me even harder to do things passionately, with my learning and my inner-self making me more able to do a lot of things that I was missing out on. I started exercising; eventually realizing the fact that my mother had told me that I should utilize this time for myself and for my growth. That helped me understand that while Abeer was not with me, I should look at the positives rather than the negatives with a plan of having him someday soon. I was prepping myself to be capable for him. Thank you, Mom, for giving this kind of energy exchange to help strengthen me. It's difficult to convey my entire situation and how I coped with it, but Yes!! My mother deserves full credit for guiding me through this phase, showing me the route to establishing my core, leading me through every phase that came my way, and assisting me in tackling it all with zeal.

I love you, Mom; without you, I am nothing… I am well aware that if not now, I'll have my Abeer with me for the rest of my life. I will keep the faith and hope you have in me burning. You are and will continue to be my strongest ally. While coping with all this emotional turmoil, I continued to learn and refine my HR expertise while the lectures were ON.

CHAPTER 14
MANGO TREE TRUST

"There are no seven wonders of the world in the eyes of a child. There are seven million.

- Walt Streightiff

Abeer was not with me since Anay had distanced him from me. There were no hearings as such because the court was seeking a response from Anay for withholding Abeer and not telling the court what he intended to do with the same concurrently on the position of this relationship as he had not provided any reply to my allegations on him. He had neither proved anything nor replied to the court about his standing on the matter. I had submitted an application to have my kid on the festival of Diwali, which Anay flatly denied, refusing to allow me to have Abeer.

The days were difficult. Moreover, I knew Anay was hurting me on purpose, and more specifically because Abeer's birthday was approaching, which was on, Children's Day. Finally, with no basis for expecting Anay to behave since he had refused to cooperate, the judge granted me a court order to have Abeer for four days. I was certain this time because of the court order against Anay and he was forced to hand Abeer over to me.

I was feeling terrible about not having my child with me on his birthday and having to return him in only four days. I don't know how to describe this feeling of love. His stay with me was only going to last four days when all I wanted was to be with Abeer forever. Obviously, I adore him wherever he is, but... I don't know how to phrase it… It was the worst sensation in the world.

I didn't want 14th November to be a dull day in my life; not even in my wildest imagination had I thought that I would see myself crying and sobbing on my child's birthday. It occurred to me that I had discussed with Anay that for Abeer's birthday, I wanted to donate something to the orphanage children in honor of Abeer's birthday and also because it was Children's Day.

I thought about it and decided to fulfill that wish for Abeer. I googled about trusts and orphanages where I could help children and found **Mango Tree Trust**, which was near my house. It was a charitable trust that provided education and basic needs to underprivileged children. I called them and explained my predicament. I am grateful to Girija for understanding my feelings and allowing me to attend on November 14 to spend time with the children and participate in the Children's Day Function. I was overjoyed and delighted to offer those kids my sign of love and to rediscover my pleasure through them. When I told my mother about it, she instantly agreed to assist me in getting items for them. She was as pleased and enthusiastic as I was.

I went shopping with my mother for some cream biscuits, ordered cake for the next day's distribution, and bought some stationary as well as drawing books and crayons for the kids. While I was ready to meet the children, I missed Abeer. I couldn't sleep all night. I couldn't stop crying.

Children's Day

My mother and I picked up the cake from the cake store in the morning, and the other items were pre-packaged the day before to be handed over to the children. Around 10:30 a.m., we arrived at the location. The kids had arrived, and the teachers had gotten me engaged in the games and other activities scheduled for the day. Overall, it was a wonderful and cheerful day for me, sharing my heart with the children and seeing my enjoyment linked to theirs. The kids were between the ages of three and five. I hugged them and sank into them, soaking up all of the feelings I desired.

It was both blissful and emotional, but it was a fruitful day filled with smiles, pleasure, and the satisfaction of having done whatever little I could for those kids. My aim was to convey Abeer to them, and I was glad to do it. After returning home, I attempted to contact my father-in-law and asked him to hand the phone over to Abeer, which he did. I wished my kid a "**Happy Birthday**" and grieved quietly, offering him flying kisses. I promised him that he would see me soon.

The 4 Days

According to the court ruling, Anay was required to hand Abeer over to me for four days, so I proceeded to Anay's house. After 3 months, I finally got Abeer. I was overjoyed. I was pulled toward him like a magnet, kissing and adoring him. We celebrated his birthday. We went to the park and had a good time while he was playing happily. We had a lovely time together, relieving the moments I had missed with him. I gave him the drawing book and crayons I had brought for the kids at the Mango Tree Trust; Abeer was sketching, reciting ABCD, and playing all day long. Four days was a really short amount of time and I couldn't really spend time with him to my heart's content. Four days flew by in a flash, and the difficult morning of saying goodbye to Abeer and handing him back to Anay seemed like a dagger ripping my heart.

I was feeling numb, unhappy, and dejected, wondering what sort of days these are where I can't have my own baby and had to give him back to Anay, who snatched him from me and placed me in this predicament; the battle for Abeer was raging in my heart. I was embracing Abeer the entire way back to Anay's home, my tears flowing like rain, my heart heavy. I handed Abeer over to Anay. My feet were shaking from despair, my heart was choking. I was back in my empty space, but what strengthened me were the days I could spend with Abeer and my part for the kids at the Mango Tree Trust.

CHAPTER 15

PERCEPTION

When I saw Anay after handing over Abeer, my heart yearned to question him about a slew of issues. I hadn't seen him since the CIBIL report disaster in August; he wasn't even attending the hearings or making any effort to correct his actions, and now Abeer was a tool for him to play with my emotions; I wanted to fire questions at him, longing for answers for making my life so difficult. Since I wasn't on speaking terms with Anay after I decided not to allow him to contact me due to his behaviour in court and refusal to allow me to have Abeer,. I felt odd staring into his eyes, the ones that had failed me. I couldn't gather the guts. to press him on the clarifications I requested.Furthermore, I felt that if I questioned him and he became aggressive, it would create a problem being there at his place, giving birth to multiple case scenarios that would land me into trouble As a result, I maintained my cool.After reaching home, I tried to recap our journey so far, the strikes that happened over the course of this dispute. I descended into the depths of my emotions, considering if I should talk to Anay only once for the purpose of Abeer, taking a step back for my child, to learn Anay's predicament in this relationship as a **LAST CHANCE**. Knowing that he had done nothing to regain my trust, giving him a chance out of the blue was a reckless decision, but I considered putting everything aside for a moment to clarify his stance. I was aware of the consequences I would face. It was obvious that I was making another emotional decision in order to protect Abeer, but it was a calculated risk to me. We had been fighting in court, blaming each other; not allowing ourselves to try to understand our true mental and emotional state. There were several instances during this conflict when I felt that I missed Anay and needed to communicate with him. I took those steps just because I wanted him to know my worth and I always expressed how much I wanted him to make things right.

I wanted to know all of this. I needed clarification for myself.

I considered contacting Anay, my pulse pounding faster while dialing Anay's phone. He took up.

"Hello, How are you?" My heart was aching.

"Good, what about you?" I answered,

He replied, *"I want to talk to you; I want to tell you many things, I miss you a lot…"* *"Please, let me speak, hear me out, and then decide whatever you wanna decide"*

That was nothing new to me because he was always saying something and doing nothing… he wore his miss you, love you on his sleeve.

"Hmm Ok," I said.

and we talked…

He spoke to me about his mistakes, how his life was without me, emotions, sentiments, fury, improvements, debts, and so on. Most crucially, he spoke about our position in this relationship. It was clearly a lot, so it didn't end it all at once… also, I didn't believe him in one go… as well. We decided to argue less and discuss each issue properly. I had contacted him to learn more about him since I was curious. I had to listen in and out of him. It was crucial to me.

First, we spoke about debts. I inquired about his debts, the specific amount (apart from the **CIBIL** report figure in case received from any other type of loan from others, etc...), and why he required so much money and couldn't share it with me. I insisted on transparency and hard facts.

Anay admitted taking those loans and that he was in deep debt, but it wasn't done on purpose. He had thought that he would manage to repay it all, but was unable to pay them because of business loss. He admitted that it was his fault since he had neglected the business, which led to financial deficit, resulting in obligations owed to agents. He couldn't deal with it all and couldn't bring himself to tell me since we were barely married; He was afraid of speaking up to me about the issue, so he chose to hide and kept lying to me to minimize the arguments, believing that he would handle things silently and that I didn't need to know about it. He went on to explain that his objective was not to damage me or breach my trust, but it continued to happen, and he had lied so much that he couldn't control the situation later on. He further said that he felt accountable for his actions.

I heard him, every word that I wished were true; I questioned him. WHY he needed to take out such a large loan in the first place? If his intention was to not hurt me, WHY did he take my jewelry all the time and use me to repay the loans, putting me in trouble, and whenever I asked about it... WHY did he assault me? It was not acceptable. I harped on, clarifying that if he was trying so hard to handle the problems silently without my involvement, WHY did he even lie to me about the issues, which ultimately got me involved, causing me trouble?

After all, he had to face the circumstances which he had always feared anyway. I understand that he had lied for legitimate reasons, but the amount of pain he had caused me while dealing with those difficulties; cheating and treating me cruelly was simply unacceptable. It was impossible for me to believe. Finally, I asked him that if he felt accountable for his actions, WHY wasn't he making any effort to fix them?

His responses did not match my inquiries, and yet he was encouraging me to believe him, despite his lack of conviction. I was willing to put up with Anay if he could regain my trust in the matter. I was willing to assist him if those difficulties were genuine, since I know that sometimes circumstances push people to act in unintended ways, but in Anay's case, it was clear that he was unwilling to do anything about it.

Second, we discussed how he intended to repay the loans and obligations; he stated that he had fully stocked the business and returned it to normalcy. Unlike before, the customer flow was quite solid, and he had compiled a list of outstanding loans and obligations. He said that he was keeping aside a specific amount of money out of daily rolling and paying the loan brick by brick while operating the business on ground levels without getting into additional trouble, making himself suitable for repaying the loan, which will take a long time but the initial start had been made. He also discussed about the land that he had decided to sell and the money that would be utilized to pay off the loans and solve the problems, providing much-needed relief.

I questioned him about the land he had promised to sell. It had been a year since he had promised to sell that land and it still wasn't sold. I understand that property deals take time, but how much effort had he put in to get it done? and it has been a year after I filed the DV case with no advancement. I questioned him HOW he had stocked the business while still straining to make loan payments. I directed him to give me loan statements from the bank so that I could check the loan amounts and the EMI's paid so far. Anay kind of retaliated by making excuses, which bothered me, so I told him that he wasn't actually doing anything to regain my trust and that he still hadn't realized my worth, because he wasn't trying to fix the distorted relationship. Instead, he was expecting me to forgive the past and accept him. I felt like I was begging him to look for solutions while he was pressing me to comprehend his dilemma and struggles. I expected him to explain less and show more through his actions.

Third, we spoke about the ongoing case and his attitude toward the whole thing, about not appearing before the court for the hearings, and causing me stress by acting up and pulling Abeer away.

He replied that it was depressing and he felt left out because he couldn't handle whatever happened after my brother's wedding. I wasn't with him for obvious reasons and Abeer was with me for 8 months. He couldn't find the grip and felt deeply remorseful whereas when he brought Abeer, he felt alive, as if someone had infused life into him and he felt at peace.

Again, his responses were just not compelling, despite my best efforts to put myself in his place and understand what he was trying to say. I can certainly understand why he felt at ease having Abeer, but why did he deprive me of him? He wouldn't allow me to meet Abeer when I went to his house to fetch my belongings. Furthermore, when the judge ordered him numerous times to bring Abeer to the court, he broke the regulations, depriving me of Abeer. I asked him about it, he said that he had reacted agitatedly to every court action because he was saddened that I wasn't talking to him and doing things through court, which was making him more aggressive; I told him that he shouldn't have reacted to the case matter that way because he had forced me to take those step because of his lies. Despite the fact that it hurt him, he should have responded fairly because he was at fault. His demeanor and actions throughout the debate were extremely unjust. He was taking it all wrong and that he had created that mess.

I listened him out, and he didn't appear to feel guilty. I chose to give myself some breathing room after covering most of the difficulties, and more importantly, I wanted time to invest my trust factor and think about it completely. Anay used to video call me and make Abeer talk to me. It was a lot of fun and felt energetic. I enjoyed sharing these wonderful times with Abeer.

I was taking my time reprimanding him and I made it plain to him that I don't trust readily. Anay was trying to convince me that he would work hard, alter his behavior, and wouldn't make the same mistakes he had made earlier. He urged me that he required my support, care, and love for things to fall into place. It was happening all at once, but I couldn't see Anay making any efforts actions to obtaining what was required and I couldn't get myself to trust him. It was just not coming from my heart; I was expected and supposed to be happy, but I was sad. I couldn't feel that positive, truthful vibe in Anay. I told him to get Abeer to me and discuss his plan of action on getting things right as the initial step and then, we shall decide further.

I also told Anay that I wouldn't be giving up on my career. He initially expressed happiness in lending me his support for my career and making things better for me and Abeer. Most importantly, he agreed to maintain transparency with me on topics that require discussion. He stated that he would handle the business carefully and engagingly, and appealed for more time to get things in order. I was focused on getting Abeer to me, and I needed a **PLAN OF ACTION.**

Anay was not a man of his words, obviously. Though his responses to my questions were strange, I was hopeful that at the very least, he would strive to change for the better now for Abeer's sake. I was on my best behavior and Anay showed his true colors. After a few days of sweet-talking, he was back in his old mindset, looking for ways to dodge the tasks I had assigned him, such as returning Abeer as the first step and discussing his plan of action, which he neither had nor meant to have. He started doubting me on petty things, like who I was in touch with, whom I contacted, and the possibility of me getting a job outside Goa. Before even getting the job, he forced me to limit myself to solely looking for jobs in Goa and kept track of every step I took. He'd turned into a stalker.

I was enraged by his cheap tactics of constantly putting me under mental stress and controlling me. I warned him not to meddle in my decisions, which caused him to become hostile and egoistic. He began calling me from unknown numbers on a daily basis, disrupting my studies and emotionally blackmailing me, saying that Abeer wanted to talk to me, but it was him who would chat on the phone. He was getting on my nerves when he used Abeer as a pawn in his cheap games.

He was playing with our emotions.

I advised him not to behave the same way as before. He sweet-talked to me about supporting me in my career, but he was not prepared for any sort of struggle required to mend this relationship. It didn't take long for me to pick up on his plan and falsehoods, and I quickly shut him up by being strong enough to inform him that I want to **DIVORCE** him. I am grateful to Ganesha for assisting me in understanding that Anay would never change. His nature of doubting, stalking, and trying to stop me from achieving anything would never change. It seemed obvious that Anay and my chapter would be over shortly.

I did not regret discovering what I discovered while going through the dispute because it was necessary for me to understand the depth of this relationship to filter out the worst for a positive outcome. It gave me the strength to battle against all difficulties and it also gave me the desire and the will to dive into this ocean and work on my life while thinking about Abeer. It taught me a lot about patience and how to regulate my emotions. I sobbed a lot for Abeer since I couldn't see him through video calls anymore, but I knew I had to have him at any cost.

I knew that the path ahead would not be smooth. I had a lot to work on by accepting the challenges that will come my way; focusing on my strengths and working on my weaknesses, my primary motto was to be happy in whatever I do. God had given me a second opportunity. I remembered what my mother had said to me. *"Check on his efforts to reclaim you and you will find out"*. It gave me power. I redirected myself back to the path I had chosen in order to fulfill my goals in life, which helped me reclaim my normalcy.

He used the words **I LOVE YOU** and **SORRY** to reassure me that things were going to improve, but certain risks are simply not worth taking, especially when those risks have failed you.

CHAPTER 16

MISSION: MéTIER

The HRM programme came to an end. I revised my résumé to reflect my HR expertise and began applying for multiple positions offered by Metier HR Services as well as other companies while waiting for a response.

I had made the choice to relocate to wherever the opportunities required. I needed to be financially independent to be able to manage Abeer's custody. I wanted to step outside my comfort zone. I did not feel at ease in this situation. I needed to feel my pulse. I wanted live independently, t feel the journey of self-discovery and manage things on my own. I wanted to explore what I was capable of, establishing predetermined norms for myself, and this time, the only dictation I heard came from myself. I was preparing myself for interviews.

Waiting, you see, is difficult, especially when there is nothing we can do to control the situation. People frequently say "I wish there was anything I could do; I feel so powerless,". They are claiming that they have no control over their circumstances. I was also in that state of **WAIT** that seemed to last forever. We may dislike waiting, but accepting and even loving it may be one of the best things we can do. God appears to have plans for our waiting periods, plans to help us grow.

"Patience is not simply the ability to wait - it's how we behave while we're waiting".

Sometimes, to have the life that is waiting for us, we must be prepared to let go of the life we have planned. I was coping with sadness; experiencing dull times, missing Abeer all the more, and sobbing. It seemed like it would never end. I was glued to my phone, hoping for a call from one of the companies I had applied to. It was a Saturday evening, and I was lying on my couch, watching Indian Idol when my phone rang. My heart skipped a beat when I read the name flashing on my phone screen. It was the company I had applied for (I had saved the phone numbers of the concerned persons when I applied for the post advertised on the portal). I answered the phone, and after the normal greetings came the big part, something I had been wanting to hear: *"We reviewed your resume, and your interview for the FIRST ROUND is scheduled at 11 a.m."*

What a breath of fresh air. I was ecstatic to prepare for the interview. My goal was to ace it.

First Round - The Telephonic Round: I was nervous and sweating, hoping for some easy questions, wanting to score high. When the interview began, I prayed to Ganesha and began answering as calmly and clearly as I could, using my knowledge and ability to give my best shot. The interview was lengthy, with all potential HR questions and practical scenarios to answer. I felt convinced that I had done a great job. The interviewer affirmatively provided input on my performance and insight into the areas I needed to focus on. He also provided feedback on the interview to the relevant department, which would coordinate with me on having me for the SECOND ROUND. Being selected for the second round, my excitement skyrocketed. It gave me a sense of accomplishment for having arrived at this point of relief and for the time and effort I had put into learning and studying the course. The significance of the effort I had put in to reach this moment.

I was checking my phone constantly, waiting again for my heart to skip a beat. After a few days, I received the call I was anticipating from the concerned department, which shared details with me for the second round, a face-to-face interview.

The next thing I knew, I was on my laptop, looking up flight tickets to Pune; I wish I had wings. I wanted to fly to Pune right then and there. I immediately booked my tickets from Indigo Airlines for three people; this time, my parents were flying with me; I thought about tagging them along since they longed for a change; they were also going through difficult times, and I wanted to give them a break from their routine. I had scheduled our tickets in such a way that we could have a day to rest before the interview since it was a late night flight; we needed a day to unwind and for me to prepare for the interview. My mother was overjoyed since she enjoys traveling and promptly made plans to visit **Shreemant Dagdusheth Halwai Ganpati** Mandir and other places. After that, I prepared my documents and began packing, ready to hit the city yet again. We stayed at a hotel near the company after arriving in Pune to get to the interview sooner.

The next morning, as planned, we headed to Dagdusheth Mandir for darshan; it was crowded as usual, as it is a popular tourist attraction in Pune. I spent some peaceful time at the temple, thanking God for the opportunity and for giving me and my family the strength to go through it all; I felt a sense of satisfaction looking back at all the challenges I'd overcome to reach this point, inch by inch. Because of our faith, we kept growing and continuing through everything. I was praying for strength and blessings for the next day's interview, hoping to be able to score well and ace it to proceed to the next chapter of my life. We grabbed our lunch locally and then strolled around the city before returning to our hotel late in the evening. I rested and prepared for the interview the next day.

Second Round - The Technical Round: The interview was scheduled for 10:30 a.m., so I arrived at the office at 9.30 a.m., an hour early. I didn't want to be late, even though it was just 28 minutes away from the hotel given the traffic and cab experience.

I was waiting in the lobby. The receptionist inquired about my purpose. I stated to her that I'd come for the interview. She handed me an interview application form to fill out with information about my family background, preferred location, basic details, previous employment and experience details, qualifications, courses, and so on, along with a résumé. I filled all the necessary information and submitted it at the reception desk while waiting for my call.

I was called to the meeting room for my interview at 10:45 a.m. I was asked about my knowledge of the position applied for and the domain I was about to work on; I explained about the same to the best of my ability and the skills I was taught during my course with Metier HR services; I did get confused and felt lost at some of the questions; call it anxiety or lack of preparation, but I managed to score decently. The reviewer identified the important areas for improvement and qualified me for the THIRD ROUND.

Third Round - The Managerial Round: This round was relatively easy because the domain knowledge questions had already been answered and scored; this round concentrated on my persona and general questions related to my personally identifiable information, hobbies, interests to assess how well I could be an asset to the company based on my interpersonal skills, communication, and professionalism, as well as how committed I am to contributing to the organization. I aced it without any unnecessary sugarcoating since I knew how crucial this opportunity was for me and how focused I was on my career development path vis-á-vis. I stated my writing as a passion and that I was ready to launch mybook.

I also explained the dispute that was going on, but I was determined not to allow my personal life interfere with my professional development by expressing my resolution in the matter. It was a captivating session that propelled me to the FOURTH and FINAL ROUND; the HR Round.

Fourth Round - The HR Round: The realization that I had been selected sank in; I was relieved after having performed well. Now my only task was to understand my salary structure negotiations after a few basic introductory questions. The HR inquired about how shortly I could join, explaining about the joining formalities. Following a discussion, we decided the date of joining. We also discussed the induction training course which will be held on the day of joining and submissions of the required documents. I thanked the HR for the opportunity and promised to do my best.

After clearing all of the rounds, I returned to the hotel feeling satisfied to have moved one step closer to my goal. I told my parents everything about the interview sessions; but they had already figured it out as happiness was evident on my face; they were happy and became tearful, recalling my hardships so far... A great sigh of relief, a sense of success and contentment. I thanked "**Ganesha**," my power, who has and will continue to shower his blessings on me. I am grateful to my parents for their unwavering support, and to my trainer, Mr. Milan Surana, for his efforts in imparting the knowledge required to be an HR professional as well as for his incredible teaching skills.

We ordered our lunch in the room and napped for a bit; we hadn't booked our return tickets owing to the interview pattern. We booked our tickets back to Goa now that the interview was over. It was a midnight departure, so we opted to check out early as we had no further plans to remain in Pune. We finished packing, completed the checkout procedures, had dinner at the hotel, and hired a cab to the airport.

It was a lovely trip, started with the intention of making the most of it. Sitting by the window seat and watching the lights glister as the plane took off gave me the confidence to fly high and aspire higher. The sky's the limit for me. I put in my earplugs and fell asleep until my mom woke me up at the announcement from the air hostess that we had arrived at our destination, but I was yet to arrive at my destination. However, I was preparing myself for the fresh beginning that was waiting for me with open arms, the feeling that 2023 will be **MY** year.

I couldn't hold back my emotions as I finally took a step closer to getting my Abeer back; the hope that had been blazing in my heart all this time was now taking shape. Now I had a plan that was ready to be executed. The silent tears I had shed were ready for closure.

I was about to shift to Pune. I just had a few days left to stay at home; the time had arrived to break free from my comfort bubble and experience life's challenges in a whole new city. I began gathering my belongings for my final packing, making a list of the essential things and searching for a location close to my office. My parents were concerned for me as I would be away, but they were also pleased, especially my mother, who had encouraged me to shape my career and achieve my objectives. They were my pillars of support, and without them, I would not have been able to instill a feeling of responsibility in regaining my lost confidence.

Finally, I thought of appreciating those who didn't believe in me. Sometimes it is good to have such folks around to teach you important life lessons. By doubting my abilities, they eventually made me believe in myself; for constantly demotivating me in every way every time I sought to do something good for myself, which made me recognize my own potential to accomplish what I set out to do. I was developing confidence in pursuing the path that was destined for me, defining and working toward my goals, overcoming every hurdle that emerged. It just pushed me a bit farther; it made me even more determined to carve out a space for myself.

Every day is a lesson! **"People"** being the hardest subject

I wouldn't call this a success yet since I'm still a work in progress and there's a lot to do in this process; this was merely a milestone achieved.

#unstoppable :-)

CHAPTER 17

NEW BEGINNINGS - [i]

"Life has got all those twists and turns. You've got to hold on tight and off you go."

- Nicole Kidman

2023…

ONE STEP AT A TIME

Here's wishing everyone a Happy New Year. I had a feeling this would be the finest year of my life; there was something incredibly positive about a fresh start.

I had completed my entire packing. We also were able to find a place to stay in Pune. My start date was January 9th. Given the weight restrictions, the luggage was too much for me to schedule a flight, so we had our driver drop us in Pune.

My parents came along to drop me off. It was a weekend, we left early in the morning to arrive early; I felt a feeling of a hollowness within me as I left my house. I was sad; missing Abeer; it was such a difficult moment I can't express; the greatest part was that I was on my path to do something for him, to be independent and to be able to claim custodial rights. We started the journey, and I slept in the car because I am a sloth bear. We stopped for lunch in Kolhapur and then continued without stopping until we arrived in Pune late in the evening.

On Sunday morning, my mother helped me with unpacking and organizing my belongings. After we were done we drove to visit my brother, who lives in Pune itself. We had a great time over lunch and discussed my work profile and other things promising we would visit each other during weekends. It was a lovely day altogether.

Monday mornings can be tough, but this one was particularly challenging as it was time for my parents to head back home. I was overwhelmed with emotions. I sought strength and focus from Ganesha, the Hindu god of beginnings and obstacles. I took blessings from my parents, touching their feet and assuring them that their trust in me will never waver. My mother hugged me tightly as she wept. They drove me to the office as we said our goodbyes and made plans to see each other again soon. As I stepped into the office, my heart was racing with a mix of emotions. Starting something new after a long hiatus can be daunting, but I was determined to make it happen. Life is about creating yourself, not just finding yourself. I was on a journey to create my own path. It takes courage to be true to yourself and follow your heart. That's why people say you're one of a kind. #Follow your heart not the crowd.

The first step was the induction process, which included filling out several forms provided by the HR department, followed by a presentation by the organization's management team about the organisation, its policies, clientele, and the facilities available to employees. The code of conduct and the basics. It was driven by people from the departments, with a test to determine the employee's knowledge of the organisation and general IQ. The documents were submitted. Regarding the induction, feedback was welcomed. The new hires were then assigned to their respective departments for training. I was saddened by the part of the form where I had to check the columns: Married, Unmarried, Divorcee.

I've come a long way, and I know such columns make my heart feel empty, but I have to fill them with the battles I won without hesitation, facing the truth of my life that I am proud of.

A **YES** to happiness and **GOODBYE** to drama and toxic people in my life.

Bless me with Strength.

More power to me!

The journey has provided me with so much growth that nothing can keep me from having what I deserve and desire.

Nothing brings me down, the sweetest note from my Aunt Mrs. Seema Prabhu while I was leaving for Pune to begin my new chapter. You are a plethora of happiness.

CHAPTER 18
A HOME
AWAY FROM HOME

The pain will end. The tears will stop. The doors will open.
A season of miracles and blessings is coming your way.
Don't give up.

- Vivek Thakur

My alarm was set off around 6.30 a.m. I already missed being at home, in my room, the space that provided me with warmth. I missed mom's ready-made breakfast, and I missed Abeer even more; it was soon 7.22 a.m. I rolled out of bed after taking a deep breath. I showered, dressed, heated some milk with Muesli, and headed to work. Being in an unknown city forces you to discover your true potential… I was no longer in my element. I was constantly on the move, whether it was for breakfast, hiring a cab to get to work on time, planning what to eat for lunch and dinner, managing my money, or even finding a housemaid, which is the most difficult task on the planet.

I was in a whirlwind, with no time to pause and reflect, I had to make swift and smart decisions while navigating the new surroundings during my initial days in Pune. But as the saying goes, "God helps those who helps themselves". I was blessed to encounter the perfect people, in the ideal place and at the precise moment, everything fell into place effortlessly, as if fate had conspired to make my transition smooth. The people I met were incredibly helpful in getting everything done quickly, and soon it felt like second nature to me.

The days were pleasant they were the best. I was happy because I was doing the career I had always wanted to do; I love HR and the functions that go with it, so the amount of dedication I was putting into my work gave me a sense of satisfaction. I adapted quickly to office life, making new friends and colleagues, learning new skills, and carrying out my daily responsibilities. I wanted to be constantly on the edge. I wanted to arrive at the highest point on the learning curve. It was one of the best phases I had earned in a long time.

I'd like to thank the department's manager, **Mr. Pankaj Bankar**, for encouraging me to do my best and for assisting me in regaining my focus whenever I was feeling down. It takes a lot of faith to have someone on board who is starting from scratch. It was more than just work for me; it was a responsibility to never disappoint the trust that he had placed in me. Thank you, sir, for being so kind and giving me the confidence to set higher goals.

That's the thing when you're busy, you're not susceptible to an emotional roller-coaster; it pushes your thoughts aside until you get home from work, and then the thoughts start worrying you about what will happen next. I began to feel the same way. before coming to Pune. I discussed the next steps with my lawyer. The legal system is extremely slow. I had no choice but to wait until the hearing at the end of January.

Both Pune and my work life were sending me positive vibes, and I was confident that everything would fall into place. I was discovering myself, going to new places, meeting new people, and challenging myself every step of the way, managing my state of being without Abeer, crying, wiping them away, and starting over. When I saw a kid of his age, my eyes filled with tears thinking about what my Abeer must be doing; the fact that I couldn't contact Anay was that he would never understand my plight given that he was the one who had put me through this and besides, he was stalking me in every way he could try to make my life more difficult and toxic. It was disheartening, even though I was now immune to his behaviour, it still caused me pain. I intended to keep my patience and cool intact. I was happy at work and inclined toward the goals I had set for myself. I was fearless because I believed in myself and my ability to relocate to another location and live my life independently. Since I had never lived alone in another city before, this was an appealing challenge.

I'm grateful for what transpired between Anay and me. Thanks to him for putting me through this, which eventually made me strong enough to seek beyond my capabilities and uncover this courage within me. Having taken Abeer away from me proved to be a turning point in my life, the vulnerability that gave me the confidence to put my inner strength to the test, from learning to drive to deciding on a career path, pursuing it, landing a job and moving to another city.

The journey was a roller coaster of emotions, but every step was worth it. I stand at a turning point in my life, the outcome of the conflict is uncertain. Though the challenges persisted, I was ready to tackle them head-on. In many ways, 2022 was a transformative year; it gave me the courage to make bold decisions. I made the most out of the year in every way possible; I emerged stronger and more self-assured. The metamorphosis continues as I gear up to confront the dispute with Anay and the situation with Abeer.

I remember how terrible the agony was when Anay tried to apologise to me; He continues to try and say that he has changed and that he will correct his actions and behavior but, his actions repeatedly hurt me enough that I realised it didn't matter anymore because emotions aren't machine-made. You cannot be healed by the person who broke you. I didn't expect Anay to bring the broken pieces of my life back together again. Why would you put your trust in someone who can betray and destroy you?

It was now or never.

Whatever happens, happens for a reason. Believe in it during the good times, and believe it even more during the bad. Belief can not only make the bad look good, but it can also make the good feel better and, in some cases, change the bad into good.

On that note, here are some obvious questions for the universe to answer.

When will the conflict be resolved? Will the divorce take place? Will I be granted custody of Abeer? Will Anay ever change? What other surprises await me?

I'm sure you're all curious about what happens next. It will almost certainly be answered soon. Until then, I'm hoping for your love and blessing.

This is Meera signing out to return to meet you all as I continue to take such leaps of faith in my unfinished life journey, with twists and turns to turn the pages of my life.

Turn your Pain into Power.

To Be Continued...

SELF-DISCLOSURE
OF THE AUTHOR

Through the struggles, I learned the art of humility. I wiped away my own tears and offered myself words of encouragement. The road was not easy and still isn't, my thoughts often clouded with pain and hurt. Some nights, I would retreat into myself, refusing to let anyone in. I struggled with trust, constantly questioning and searching for evidence before allowing myself to believe in anything or anyone. I was not always filled with joy and positivity, but what kept me going was my faith, my determination not to play the victim, and my inner strength that refused to give up on myself.

There are these beautiful words said by Surbhi Pandey which stuck with me **"positive thinking does not work all the time, taking the right action with the right mindset and understanding why you are doing what you are doing works"**. I have no regrets because the actions I took were guided by a lot of channelled thoughts and led me to a constructive life I could never have imagined.

I am grateful to Ganesha for providing me with opportunities to grow. Manage my conflicts. This year, I met my most broken, but also my strongest, self. I am grateful for my struggle because it allowed me to discover my inner strength. Moving on is never about forgetting what happened, but rather about trying to recall it without feeling a pang in your chest. Many things crushed my heart but restored my vision. I am proud of the woman I am growing into… My perspective has shifted. My mindset has shifted. My level of tolerance has shifted. Yes, I have evolved!

- Be Real or Be Gone.

- I Love People Who Gossip Behind My Back, That's Exactly Where They Belong, Behind My Back.

LIFE LESSONS

- Every day, I am learning to let the distance between where I am and where I want to go inspire rather than frighten me.

- Take yourself out of the situation. Consider yourself an observer. Fix or let go. Not everything is meant to be saved. Not everything is meant to be fully explored.

- Sometimes in life you have to suffer, not because you were bad, but because you didn't know when to stop being good.

- The job, the party, the relationship knowing when to leave is so important. Do not stick with a toxic environment.

- Fitting in will make you unhappy, be your own uncool weird self and whoever still wants to hang around you. Keep them close.

- Expecting honesty from those who lie to themselves is unreasonable. It's an expensive gift, cheap people cannot afford it.

- At any minute, there is someone who can come along and change your life. That person is you. Believe in your heart and soul that you are capable of doing great things in life. You are the only thing that is getting in your path.

- Cut the ties that are harming your heart, mind, and spirit.

- When you completely trust someone without reservation, one of two outcomes occurs:

a) A LIFE PERSON
OR
b) A LIFE LESSON

MY PARENTS ARE MY HOME

"Parents are living gods. They do everything to make their children happy and expect nothing in return."

\- Saravana Kumar Murugan

My father, **Mr. Deepak Narayan Kesarkar**, has never failed to express his love for us. He is not the sort of person who says things or expresses a definite NO. He is the sort of person who will speak less and act more in any decision he makes, whether it is buying a home, or a car, or making crucial business decisions. He's a true achiever. His actions always spoke louder than his words. He wants to be understood and avoids boasting. You'd best have that much patience if you're dealing with my father because he's a tough nut to crack.

He is a great example of an actual struggle. He had just about nothing since his parents were struggling to make ends meet. They lived in "**Bhedshi,**" a village in the Maharashtra state. When my father turned 16, he began selling onions and potatoes on the streets of Bhedshi. The journey from a vendor to a successful businessman was challenging, with highs and lows, but he never gave up. He pursued his dream of growing his business and opening his own grocery store, and he was fortunate. My mother **Mrs. Neeta Kesarkar** deserves a great deal of credit for supporting him along the path towards achieving his goals. It was difficult for her to understand every move he made, but she silently backed him and trusted in him. Faith is what makes a person successful in everything they do;

this is what an ideal partner is meant to be; this is what marriage feels like, supporting each other during the struggle while still being happy.

He never disappointed my mother or betrayed her unwavering trust. The effort required to be an achiever was immense, and if I start writing, it will certainly be a book, therefore I am cut short.

He's constructed this world for himself and us with a lot of patience. my parents shared equal responsibility for everything involving me and my brother. They were always approachable to us and offered us their time and attention. We used to sit in the hall together before our school reopened, and dad used to put covers on our notebooks. I cherish these little moments when I reflect on them. Every year a new bag, every birthday new clothes, and he made certain that there was nothing from his end that we would be unhappy with. With a slew of other amazing experiences.

We moved from Bhedshi to Goa for education because our parents were constantly concerned about our future and did not want us to face the same difficulties that they faced; they wanted us to receive a good education so that we can face the challenges that have shaped us into who we are today. Thank you is a simple word, and all I can do for them is make them happy and love them forever. They deserve a lot.

My father has been my rock throughout this tumultuous journey. Despite the chaos of the world and my own struggles, he has remained steadfast and unwavering in his support for me. It is not an easy task for a parent to witness their child's marriage fall apart and to watch them struggle to pick up the pieces, especially when that child was handed over in perfect trust, only to be mistreated and hurt. But my father has been there for me every step of the way, and for that, I am eternally grateful. My father refused to allow me to return to Anay unless he showed, proved, and made steps to make one for his hurtful actions. He is a man of strong principles; he has always carried himself with dignity and has never compromised his self-esteem. I know what I've accomplished by believing in myself and maintaining my identity. It's a proud moment for him to witness me breaking down all the barriers and recognising how far I've come and how far I still have to go.

My mother was always there for me emotionally she gave me the strength to confront the enormous challenge that lay ahead of me. She smiled at me to make me feel less helpless. Every morning, however, I observed how many tears they shed for me and how vulnerable they became. My father was well aware that this was not only my battle, but also his; he was concerned about how I would handle it all, and he made certain that I would not have to face it alone. I count myself exceedingly lucky to have such parents that never give up on their children. I am a princess because I am the daughter of a king who protects me continuously and has made tremendous sacrifices to secure my happiness.

We, adults, criticize our parents when they don't understand us or make a mistake, but we forget how many times they must have reprimanded us in love when we were kids, then forgotten and held us in love without bringing it up again. I'd like to apologize to my parents for blaming them and saying things to them both intentionally and unintentionally. Their love and sacrifices have provided me with a life of abundance and fulfillment, and all I can offer in return is a little time, attention, understanding, care, and respect. They are the foundation upon which I stand tall in the world.

I owe them everything.

ACKNOWLEDGEMENTS

I thank my "**Ganesha**" in any situation, no matter how bad it was; his mission was stronger than my problems. He provided me with the power to overcome any challenges that came my way in order to meet myself in a completely new way. I am confident I will learn from this experience since I enlist the help of my "Ganesha" in all I do.

Thank you very much, **Deepak** and **Neeta Kesarkar** (Parents): For inspiring me to believe that I can achieve anything and everything in life, for sticking with me through this, and for aiding me in keeping steadfast in my decision. It would not have been possible without your unflinching support. The equally Strong, courageous, patient, loving, and caring.

Thank you very much, **Mstr. Abhiraj** (son): For putting up with me, for being such a nice child, even on the days when you became angry, sullen, disobedient, and nostalgic; what more could I wish for from a three-year-old at this terrible time; for genuinely being my strength and stress buster. I love you.

Mr. Shubham Kesarkar (Brother): Thank you for your support at this tough period. You will always have a special place in my heart and for being an eye opener at times. Thank you!

Mrs. Shivanee Kesarkar (Sister-in-law): Thank you for always motivating me and making me see the bigger picture of standing firm in any given situation.

Thank you so much, **Mrs. Seema Prabhu** (Aunt): for your assistance during these trying times in our lives. It is greatly appreciated.

Mrs. Meena Kulkarni (Aunt): You always have been the greatest support. Thank you so much for all of your helpful advice.

Mrs. Girija Candolkar & Mrs. Siddhi Morajkar - Mango Tree Trust: Thank you, Girija and Siddhi, and the entire faculty, for allowing me to be a part of the Children's Day function for letting me spend time with the kids and offering them my love; understanding my feelings. It means a lot to me. As I continue to share my love with the children at Mango Tree Trust.

Mr. Milan Surana - HR Trainer & Motivational Speaker, Metier HR Services: I cannot express how grateful I am. You are an inspiration to many and me; you helped shape my career and believed in me on my most vulnerable days. You have the power to boost my self-esteem and motivate me to believe in myself.

Mr. Pankaj Bankar - Manager, Paysquare Consultancy Limited: Thank you so much, sir, for being so understanding and supportive on all levels. for giving me the opportunity to work on my goals and for assisting me in making my mark. This is totally incredible. I am fortunate to be a part of your team and fortunate to have a manager like you in my professional life.

Friends: Ankita.K, Amey, Ankita.N, Kedar, Parisha, and Vibhav make up our "kaden gang". The reason for this is that our plans never worked out when we planned get together; instead, they worked when we made random on-the-spot plans. I know it is hilarious, but that is just how it is. Thank you very much! For having my back; for always being there for me.

This friendship will always be special. **Parisha**: I remember you saying once that I write so well, so creatively, *"why don't you write a book?"* and when I shrugged, you said, *"Why not? You absolutely can and should"*. It stayed with me. You left a mark on me.

Mr. (Adv.) Sachin Desai, Thank you for taking on my case. You are the top legal counsel, I am confident that we have the best chance of winning the case, and with your powerful intellect, this will come true. Because truth cannot be defeated, and KARMA is a bitch.

Mr. Abbas Shaikh (Father's Friend), I am grateful for this friendship.

Your advice meant a lot to me. Nothing makes me happier than knowing you are there for us at this tough time.

Thank you, **BlueRose Publications**, and everyone on my publishing team, for your interest in my story. The sheer dedication to getting my book published. This is specific: **Ms. Rashika**, the Publishing Consultant, the extremely helpful. **Ms. Deepika** and **Ms. Saloni**, my dedicated Publishing Managers; **Ms. Mansi**, my brilliant Editor; **Ms. Muskan**, the best Graphic Designer; **Mr. Rohit**, the very talented Typography Designer; the **Marketing Team** and everyone else who helped make this book possible. It has been a pleasure working with you all.

Finally, but not least, Thank you to everyone who pitched in small and large ways in lessening my pain and putting a smile on my face during this challenging time.

ABOUT THE AUTHOR

Divya Kesarkar, a Scorpion born in July. Graduated from St. Xavier's College in Mapusa, Goa, with degrees in Psychology and Sociology. She also holds a Diploma in Aviation, Hospitality and Travel management from the Frankfinn Institute of Air Hostess Training. She started her career as a Human Resource Professional with Métier HR Services and currently works at Paysquare Consultancy Limited, Pune.

Writing is her passion! She began writing as a hobby, never intending to one day publish a book. She was chosen as one of the top 100 authors in Hashtag Kalakar's Creative Writing Competition. One of her writings was featured in Hashtag Kalakar's magazine, along with a certificate stating the All India Ranking. She swears by the quote "This Too Shall Pass" by Abraham Lincoln. She enjoys travelling, listening to music, driving, and expressing joy through her painting occasionally.

Her debut book **Turn The Page**, is about discovering herself in the midst of personal complexities and life. Turning her Pain into Power- The story that transformed her into an unstoppable woman.

Write to her on Instagram: @div4_7

9 789357 049351